T0131539

JAKE FADES

*A Novel
of Impermanence*

DAVID GUY

Trumpeter
Boston & London
2008

Trumpeter Books
An imprint of Shambhala Publications, Inc.
Horticultural Hall
300 Massachusetts Avenue
Boston, Massachusetts 02115
www.shambhala.com

Printed in the United States of America

⊗ This edition is printed on acid-free paper that meets the
American National Standards Institute z39.48 Standard.
♻ Shambhala Publications makes every effort to print on recycled
paper. For more information please visit www.shambhala.com.
Distributed in the United States by Random House, Inc.,
and in Canada by Random House of Canada Ltd

Designed by James D. Skatges

THE LIBRARY OF CONGRESS CATALOGUES THE PREVIOUS EDITION OF THIS BOOK
AS FOLLOWS:

Guy, David, 1948–
Jake fades: a novel of impermanence/David Guy.—1st ed.
p. cm.
ISBN 978-1-59030-433-4 (hardcover)
ISBN 978-1-59030-566-9 (paperback)
1. Priests, Zen—Fiction. 2. Bar Harbor (Maine)—Fiction.
3. Impermanence (Buddhism)—Fiction. I. Title.
PS3557.U89J35 2007
813'.54—dc22
2006035725

Practice secretly,
working within as though a fool,
like an idiot.

—Tozan Ryokai,
"Song of the Jewel Mirror Samadhi"

Denizens of Central Square in Cambridge, Massachusetts, will notice that, though this novel takes place in the present day, I describe a donut shop on Mass. Ave. that is no longer there. As a resident of Cambridge from the early nineties, I simply can't imagine the square without that shop. That fact suggests that this is a Central Square of the imagination—not of reality—as it certainly is. That goes for all the characters as well.

For their suggestions on my manuscript, I would like to thank Beth Guy, Sarah Jane Freymann, Giles Anderson, Tom Campbell, and the editorial staff at Shambhala Publications, especially the intrepid Dave O'Neal, who brought the staff's suggestions forward and worked on the book with me. I'm sorry I'm so stubborn and don't take suggestions well. You should try being married to me (as one of you did).

Thanks to Alma Blount for her tireless support of my writing, and for dragging me off to my first meditation class.

I would also like to thank the staff of Charlie's Tap in Cambridge for their invaluable aid during my early weeks of studying meditation. Without their assistance I could never have continued.

And my deepest thanks go to my two wonderful teachers, Larry Rosenberg and Taitaku Pat Phelan.

DG

JAKE FADES

1

"WHAT'LL IT BE, FATHER?" the bar girl said.

"He's not that kind of priest," I said.

"There are kinds now?" somebody said.

"There's more in the world than those Irish micks you've spent your life confessing to," another guy said.

"I haven't been to confession in years."

"It would take two days, and he can't get the time off."

"Guinness," Jake said. He seemed to enjoy the repartee.

"I'll have a Harp," I said. "The ale."

Jake did look like a priest, one of those Franciscan friars you see in old movies; he wore his gray *hipari*, those Japanese jackets that look vaguely clerical, and he always wore a turtleneck, always black. The man didn't have a shred of affectation, but always wore the same clothes, as if they were his uniform. It was more like he didn't want to bother with choices. He topped it off with a black beret.

It was the bald head that really did it. There was only a little white hair on the fringes but he shaved that too, totally slick, shiny in the lights. He had a round little shape, diminished stature; he looked like a medieval monk, always smiling.

"What kind of priest is he?" asked somebody a couple stools down.

"Buddhist," I said. "Zen."

"What do they call them?"

"Sensei," the guy beside me said, an intense little bird who kept pushing up his glasses. "Roshi."

You never know who might show up in a Cambridge bar. Scholars of all sorts.

"Jake," the man himself said. "Call me Jake."

"Father Jake, then. It's got a ring to it."

"I'm calling him Padre," the bar girl said, bringing the beer. "I've always wanted to call somebody that. He's so cute!" She leaned over. "Let me see that little head." She took it in her hands and Jake obligingly leaned forward; she planted a kiss smack in the middle. The place broke into a cheer.

"She never kisses my head," somebody said.

"Or gives you any, for that matter."

"Dream on, boys," she said. "You'll never be this cute."

Cute he may have been, but this was a man who had spent years in one of the severest temples in Japan, often sitting in meditation for hours every day. Before that he'd been an art student, cab driver, mechanic; he could still take apart any machine you put in front of him, find what ailed it, and put it back together. After Japan he'd bummed around and finally settled in Maine, where he didn't seek students—they just seemed to find him, like yours truly.

So he might have looked like one of the seven dwarfs, but he was hard-assed and tough-minded. He could have gone back to those sittings in Japan right now. When I first knew him, round shape and all, he could lead my son and me on long bike rides, scale the steepest hills, and leave us in the dust.

The bar girl was quite a piece of work herself, dressed as black as any Zen student; all the girls there seemed to be, I don't know whether it was a policy of the place or what. She had on a short black top with a skirt, which happened to be leather and rather short itself. The top seemed small and tight, blown out by some major boobs, and her hair, short

2

like the top and skirt, was streaked in purple. There were umpteen little rings in her ear, a larger one in her nose, and nail polish to match the hair streaks; she was also clopping around on platform shoes, all but walking on stilts, every step an adventure.

She looked washed out and hung over, as if she'd just rolled out of bed—possibly in those same clothes—though it was almost dinnertime. And she had that trembly little edge that I associate with migraine sufferers, smiling but with a little tremor so you had the feeling that if there was a loud sound she'd shatter into pieces, an arm would fall off, something.

"What's your name, sweetheart?" Jake said.

I'd seldom known him to be so gallant.

"Jessica," she said. "Jess."

"Jess the mess," some guy down the bar said.

"Sit on it," she said, holding up her thick middle finger, dabbed with purple. "Rotate."

She smiled at Jake, who was beaming right back. "He'd probably like it," she said.

"I prefer Jessica," he said.

"That'll be fine, Padre."

"A little action, Jess?" A guy down the bar held up his glass.

"In your dreams," she said. "But I'll get you a drink."

I'd never known the old boy to be a bar hound; we had the stuff around, and he took a nip before he went to bed, maybe had a cold one after a day in the sun. But almost as soon as we got to town and stopped at the Y to drop our stuff, he said, "There's a place back on Green Street, quite relaxing. You can't hang out at the Y. But this is perfect. No pretensions."

I'd spent some time around in Boston and Cambridge myself, what with my son down there, and every bar had its crowd. Irish, blacks, Chinamen, you were always on somebody's turf, and of all the drunken, aggressive, angry bar-fight towns I've ever seen, Boston was the worst. Everybody had a chip on his shoulder.

But this place was different; leave it to Jake to find it. The adjacent room was an award-winning restaurant with a Jamaican cook in an open kitchen who always seemed to be high on something, juggling pans and clattering around, flames shooting everywhere. But he nevertheless had a knack; even a slender fish filet came out perfect. All kinds of fancy people walked down that little alley to eat.

The bar crowd, weirdly, had nothing to do with the restaurant. They couldn't afford it, most of them, grad students taking forever with their dissertations, guys who worked with computers, the two guys down the street who closed their filling station at five, post office workers, a couple of writers, city hall bureaucrats. It was all the guys left out of all the other bars. For that very reason they got along.

"You guys from the neighborhood?" It was the guy beside me again, the one who had known the Japanese titles, a thin, dark, intense guy with large black glasses that kept sliding down his nose. "There's that place toward the river."

"That's Korean. Not our style. We're from Maine."

"What brings you to town?"

"Jake's leading a retreat. Teaching some classes."

"Hank'll be leading," Jake said. "I'm watching."

You'd have thought he was off in his own world, staring down at those small thick hands as if wondering at all the work they'd done, taking a hit now and then on his Guinness. He was the most self-contained person I'd ever met. But he picked up on things.

"There'll be some disappointed people in that case," I said. I felt a nervous thrum in my belly. This was news to me.

"The man has a following," I said to the guy beside me. "Quite avid."

"Disappointed they'll have to be," Jake said.

4

Technically speaking, of course, you should be able to jump in any time. You talk off the top of your head, actually the pit of your belly, speaking from your years of experience. You don't compare your words to someone else's, just give what you have, all you have, every time.

"I might be interested," the guy said. "Can I contact someone?"

"We'll put up flyers. I'll bring some here."

A great place to publicize a Zen retreat.

It would be nearly full from Jake's following alone. He hadn't taught for months.

He drained the rest of his glass in a swallow, slid off the stool, and hit the floor. I'd been pacing with him, still had a gulp left.

"Shake hands with your teacher," he said to the young man, slapping me on the back. Quite sincerely, the guy pushed up his glasses for the tenth time and shook my hand.

"Drink up," Jake said. "I'm hungry."

Our exchange with this young man was apparently his way of telling me something.

2

WE DIDN'T HAVE MONEY TO WASTE. The tourist season was over on Mount Desert Island, so we'd done our months of work, Jake repairing bikes at the same shop where he'd worked for thirty years, me running the register, a job they gave me as a favor to him. They close up on Labor Day and head down to Fort Lauderdale, where they do the same thing, rent bikes, sell and repair them. They find some other old duffer to do repairs. Anyone can do my job.

Jake owned a house—a gift from a patron—with a capacious garage apartment. In season we lived in the apartment and rented the house. Once the tourists were gone we had a lot more space, back in the house. Also a lot more time. That's when we did our retreats.

I like both seasons. Each seems appropriate at the time.

There is a Buddhist concept called *dana*, by which students support their teachers. Jake shared what he got with me. What with Madeleine around, his oldest and most devoted student, he was set for life. About me things were less certain.

Here we were, anyway, Cambridge in autumn, the most beautiful season by far, leaves bright and spectacular on the trees and a chill to the evening air as the light faded early. It's one of my favorite spots in the world, but the prices eat you alive, hence our residence at the Y. I was actually surprised by our trip to Green Street; we could have had a beer any-where. Now we were headed up Mass. Ave. toward one of Jake's cheap eateries. He knew them all over.

He'd fallen silent. I was never sure whether he was having one of his episodes or just afraid of one. In past years he'd have been chatting away as we walked, grabbing my arm in an Old World way. He'd been a Jewish cab driver before he was a Zen teacher. But he had those brief moments of forgetting what was up, had to remember where he was, where he was headed, what he was doing, not entirely sure what would pop out of his mouth. Silence was safer.

He was still always in touch with the pace of things, what he called the "unconscious rhythm of the universe." "Don't be ahead," he would say to me. "Don't be behind. Be right on the money."

You had to feel it.

There was plenty of entertainment on Mass. Ave., a perpetual circus. Central Square was a major center for the home-less, what with a shelter nearby. They congregated on the benches, hung around the subway stop. There always seemed to be a gang in front of the Y, a rough looking crowd, tattoos on their shoulders, cigarettes in their pockets. In front of city hall were some big-bellied pols, looking useless and bewildered. Always there was the rush of traffic, nutty Boston drivers finding ways to cut people off and give them the finger.

The cheap eatery this time was up past the Y, no decor whatsoever, four little tables, rotisserie chickens in the window. That was their one entrée, and they had just a few sides, but it was delicious, just like grandma used to make. Dirt cheap. Less than the beer.

"So what's this about me being the teacher?" I said.

"Don't you want to eat first?"

"Are you afraid I'll throw up?"

We had sat down with our chicken and mashed potatoes,

peas with little pearl onions, glasses of water. Jake had taken off his beret and put it on the table, always the gentleman. He loved the ritual of sitting down. Every meal was a ceremony.

"I can eat and talk," I said. "I'll just be waiting if we don't."

"Don't wait," he said. "Eat."

"Talk and eat." We were past the Zen lessons.

He shrugged, split the leg from the thigh of his chicken. "We've got to be realistic," he said. He seemed utterly casual, as if chatting about the weather. "I don't know if I can do it."

Because of the way we lived, seasonally, Jake hadn't taught for six months. In past years he'd found a way to do weekend events, but this year he'd let it ride. Students came to see him—most lived in New England anyway—to talk and sit informally. He taught by phone, also a little by e-mail, though he didn't like that, wasn't a good typist with those thick mechanic's hands. But he hadn't given a talk in six months.

"You did fine around the shop all summer," I said.

Sometimes I would see him just sitting, parts spread in front of him on the table or floor. He might have a bewildered look, then he'd settle into a kind of calm; he'd sit and wait. After a while he'd begin working again.

"Bicycles are one thing," he said. "Machines in general. All my life, drop me in front of a machine, parts all over the place, and even if I've never seen it before, I'll get it together. Sooner or later I see it. But if I blank out in a talk, there are no parts on the floor. There's nothing."

You might have thought he'd be frustrated, angry, or sad, but he was just tearing into the chicken, that delighted little smile on his face. The leg went first, then he started on the breast.

Jake had always been a deliberate talker in the zendo, never prepared a thing. He liked to hold the *kotsu*, that little stick that priests carry, like a stake, plant it on the floor in front of him, and grip with both hands. He might pause for twenty seconds, thirty, waiting for the next point to come or the last to settle.

But last spring some of the pauses had been longer. It was as if he were trying to retrieve something way down there. Sometimes what he came up with seemed out of the blue. Zen talks are like that, make sudden leaps. But I'd wondered.

"It doesn't matter," I said. "They love what you say."

"That has its limits."

"I'm not sure it does."

"It does for me."

"It comes from the deep part of your mind. It has meaning." I honestly believed that. Anything he came up with would be helpful.

"You're not being realistic," he said. "You're not facing this."

"I am."

"I'm losing my mind."

He said that with all the emotion of someone who had lost his wallet. It was the mashed potatoes at that point; he was sitting there with that stupid little plastic fork, taking each bite with a little gravy, a cluster of peas with an onion. He was saving the thigh for last, his favorite part.

"That's an exaggeration," I said.

"Everything goes eventually. No use trying to hang on. I can watch it. It's astonishing. Something's right there, then it's gone."

"We all have that," I said.

"Not like I have it."

This was giving me a stomachache.

"Whatever happens, I'll take care of you," I said.

"I know. And I'll die before it all goes. I'm convinced."

There had been some heart problems before this, blood pressure and circulation. It wasn't just his mind.

"I won't wind up a babbling idiot," he said.

9

"I don't want you to worry."

"I'm not. But we've got these talks."

"Why did we come down here now? Of all times."

For years Madeleine had wanted to start a center in Cambridge, Jake in charge, the whole thing sponsored by her. She worshiped the ground he walked on, couldn't understand why he wouldn't make himself more accessible. Students had to schlep up to Mount Desert Island, sleep in sleeping bags, dash out in the frigid morning to a Porta-Potty. He wouldn't even record his talks.

She'd have had him speaking in Carnegie Hall. She'd rent out the place herself.

Just when I thought he should be kicking back for good, seeing people in that informal way, he told her he'd come down and have a look.

"I have two reasons," he said. "One I haven't told you. The other is this idea of the center. But that's not for me. It's for you."

"*Me?*"

"That's what I mean about being realistic. You'll take care of me. Who'll take care of you?"

The ache in my belly was deepening.

"Have you thought about it?" he said.

"Of course."

"What have you come up with?"

"Not a whole lot."

"You can't run a cash register the rest of your life. Four months a year."

"I know."

"Even if I leave you the house, which I will, there are expenses. Unless you acquire a gift for repairing bikes."

"I don't think so."

Jake had tried to teach me. I was all thumbs.

"I want you to teach. Carry this on. It's time."

In the sense that he was ready to quit, it was. In the sense that I was ready to start, no.

"Madeleine will have her center," he said. "It just won't be me."

I had, during long *sesshins*, given a talk or two. Jake had taught me various rituals. But I hadn't been in charge of anything. I'd never even led a one-day retreat.

"She doesn't want a center if it isn't you," I said.

"I'll be there at the beginning. But the woman has eyes. I'm seventy-eight years old."

"She thinks you're immortal."

"She's got to grow up."

Of all the things Jake had said, that one startled me the most. I'd never heard him say a word against Madeleine.

"Just sit with me up there," he said. "Sit at the front for the talks. Probably everything will be fine. But if I can't handle it, if it all dissolves before my eyes, I'll pass it to you."

Good Lord.

"You've got to do this," he said. "There's no other way I can handle it."

What could I say? The man had given me everything.

"I'll do it."

"Good." You'd have thought I'd told him I'd take attendance or something. It was over as far as he was concerned. His plate was empty. Literally. Not a drop of gravy left. "We've got to go up the street," he said. "There's no dessert here."

His one vice. The man was willing to give up his whole mind, thought by thought, but I'd never known him to skip dessert at any meal. We couldn't go to bed without some cake and coffee.

He'd sleep like a baby, after two cups. A little bald one.

3

SITTING BEGINS THE DAY, has for almost twenty years, and in Cambridge there are various options: the Korean place that the guy mentioned in the bar, an Insight center a couple of blocks up from the Y. One of the glitches in Madeleine's scheme is that there are already meditation centers here, but she thinks Jake is unique, and for once I agree with her. Besides, if she foots the bill, what's the difference?

But the best place to sit is right where you are. The rooms at the Y were a tad Spartan, with one of those iron bed frames that you couldn't dent with a sledgehammer, a worn-out mattress that had seen God knows what kind of action, a desk and wooden chair where you were supposed to write letters to mama back in Duluth, a battered wooden wardrobe, tiny sink in the corner. The walls were a pallid green, the bed frame darker. Jake and I carried our cushions everywhere, and I made a mat out of the blanket, sat in front of the door. Not much space in those Y rooms, and a bad smell to them, hard to describe. Hardscrabble working class. The stagnating dreams of dozens of faceless men.

Sometimes it seems that in your sleep you go to some faraway place, and you have to sit in the morning just to inhabit your body again, to know you're here. Sometimes it seems the whole thing of sitting, a whole lifetime of sitting, is just to get comfortable with having a body, as if you've spent several millennia without one, without that restriction. I've sat for over twenty years and have less idea how to do it than I ever did. It's simple when you begin, more complicated as you go on. The Buddha's teachers acknowledged him as a meditation master years before his enlightenment, but he didn't get anywhere until he started all over and sat the way he had as a child.

All I know is that it's helped me more than anything I've ever done, and that people out on the street—rushing to the subway while they gulp their coffee, shouldering people aside and cramming into the last car, staring at the floor as if waiting for something to end, they're not sure what—haven't done it. They need to.

God knows how long Jake had been up. Sometimes when we occupied the same room—the Y rooms are all singles—I'd blink awake in the morning and he'd be sitting already, right in bed, just the pillow for a cushion. He'd continue till I finished.

I knocked on his door at 8:45. We were due at Madeleine's at 10:00.

"I know the place for breakfast," he said.

I'd passed it any number of times, a battered dirty storefront called the Golden Donut, though there was an old sign that said Twin Donuts right below a newer one. The place had been taken over by a Chinese family. They should have called it Jade Donut. Though if anything was worthy of an apotheosis in New England, raised to the status of Golden (other than pilsner beer), it was the donut.

Jake hadn't been there for four months, but as soon as he entered, the tallish Asian woman at the front, thin and going gray, said, "Hi, Jake," and without missing a beat, spoke to a small woman behind her. "One light."

She turned back. "How about your friend?"

"Black," Jake said.

From then on, whenever I came in, almost before I could get to my stool, there was a cup of black coffee waiting for me.

Eggs, potatoes, toast, and that coffee were all of $2.30. Juice was another fifty cents. Jake substituted a muffin for the toast—he would—and they knew that too, waited until they brought the plate to ask what kind.

"What's fresh?" he said.

"Everything, Jake. What's the matter with you?"

The food was good; I like grease as much as the next man. But ancient grease like that has an old taste, as if it's embedded in the grill. The freshest eggs aren't right with that to flavor them. And they cook right beside the sausage and bacon. It all mixes in.

The coffee was superb. So was the corn muffin. Jake gave me a bite.

"I love this place," he said.

It was a classic Formica countertop, wound to the back in U-shapes so it could accommodate more people; the first U— where we sat—was nonsmoking, though the cloud of smoke, like the smell of grease, drifted all over the room.

The back two U's were jammed with homeless and near-homeless from all over the square. Most of them stared into a coffee cup, smoking. One, a black man who looked African, ate an omelet and spoke cheerfully to himself, making a speech. A thin pale woman wrapped in an overcoat stared around, rocking in her seat. Some guys at the back were carrying on. Otherwise the place was quiet.

"There's no bottomless cup of coffee," Jake said. "You pay for every cup. Otherwise they'd never leave."

"I believe it."

"They're not all unemployed. Some of them work in the candy factory. Necco wafers. Ever have one?"

14

"When I was a kid."

"These people made them."

I'd eaten my last Necco wafer.

"Lily knows their names. Every one. How they like their coffee. I've never seen anything like it."

As if on cue, she stepped our way.

"Who's your buddy, Jake?"

"Hank. He works with me."

"Buddhist too?"

"I guess. If I am, he is."

She put her hands together, made a little bow.

"She belongs to a Baptist church," Jake said. "Totally Chinese."

"Whole world ass backwards," Lily said.

That was for sure.

"Where you been, Jake? Haven't seen you in months."

"Up in Maine. I live in Maine. You remember."

"That's right. Live in Maine. Come down see girlfriend."

"She's not a girlfriend."

"I think might be. What you think, Hank? Jake bring her here one time. Good-looking woman."

"You've got to wonder," I said.

"Never come back. What's wrong, Jake? She no like donuts?"

Madeleine probably wasn't a real donut hound.

"She stay at home. Cook for you herself. Home cooking."

Jake was smiling. He must have really liked Lily.

"She no have sweet stuff, I bet. We got what you really want."

She had taken our plates and was wiping the counter.

"What kind of donut today, Jake?"

I stared at him. "You have a donut after that?"

"These donuts good for you," Lily said. "Try one."

"You had a muffin," I said. "You had cake last night."

"I live it up when I come to the city. This is my vacation."
He looked at Lily. "Lemon."

"Lemon good. You want lemon, Hank?"

"Why don't you have ice cream on it?" I said.

"We no do that. Straight donut here. Classic donut."

"Wouldn't want to overdo it," I said.

"Golden donut," she said.

Jake picked up his bag on the way out, as we paid.

"See you boys tomorrow," Lily said. "Jank and Hake. Easy
remember."

Apparently not. But it was her first mistake.

Jake looked back on his way out. "When I go totally dotty,"
he said, "completely out of it, I'll hang out here."

"God damn it, Jake."

He wore a big grin.

Outside it was a marvelous New England autumn morning, sky clear and sunny, the slightest chill to the air. Jake
munched his donut as we walked.

"We have plenty of time," he said. We were strolling slowly. "I hope I wasn't hard on Madeleine yesterday."

"I knew what you meant."

"She doesn't need to grow up. She needs to face this. She
hasn't faced it."

"There's a lot of that going around."

Jake had told me about Madeleine in the past; we'd had
long talks. She was the classic poor rich girl, heiress to a major
fortune, had a place in Cambridge and another in Bar Harbor.
An apartment in New York.

She'd been one of his first students back in the eighties
when he just had a sitting group and taught a class from time
to time. She wandered into the bike shop the same way I did,
saw the notice for the class. She was on her third marriage
at the time, and it was collapsing all around her. She'd been

16

to counselors, psychologists, psychiatrists. Lawyers of course. "She was suicidal," Jake had told me. "Claims I saved her. I didn't save her. Clear seeing saved her. But people get confused. They think it's you."

I knew what he meant. It wasn't him. But I also knew how she felt. Talking to Jake was like nothing else I'd ever done. Even with a shrink, the most highly skilled one, you could see the wheels turning, judgments being made, techniques worked out. Nothing wrong with that. It was their job. Some were good at it.

But talking to Jake was like throwing stones into a well. A deep, still well where you never hit bottom. There was no judgment, no thinking. A helpful word now and then. Somehow, in that situation, the things you said stayed right in front of you. You saw them in a new way. The way he was seeing them. Clearly.

There was more teaching in the way he listened than in all the words he'd ever said.

"I used to think everybody had to sit," he had told me. "Everybody needed a strong practice. But some people can't do it. They're not ready, won't be in this lifetime. You have to take them as they are."

Through the years Jake had had multiple students who came to him wanting to sit. What they really wanted, what made them feel better, was just to talk to him, throw stones down that well. He would hear them go on about how they were establishing a practice, trying to get there. After a while they would drop it, or he would drop them. There was nothing to talk about.

Except for Madeleine. She still hung on twenty-five years later.

"Did she ever come on to you?" I asked him once.

"Wanted to make me husband number four. Live in that big house. Had a meditation room all set up."

"Were you tempted?"

"It would have been the end of everything. I have to live the way I do, somehow. Besides, the husband of Madeleine Harold. No one lasts in that job."

He hadn't quite answered what I'd asked, but I didn't press him. What Lily wondered, I wondered.

The awkward thing was the money. Madeleine would happily have provided for Jake's every need. That was hardly unprecedented in the history of Buddhism; all the way back to the Buddha, there were wealthy people around. But the Buddha only let them do so much. He would take a meal, but wouldn't let them provide all the meals. He would stay in decent quarters in the rainy season, but would wander the rest of the time. The middle way, by his standards, was not all that middle. The Cambridge Y would have looked posh to him.

Madeleine had given Jake the house on Mount Desert Island; nothing in the life he had led would have accumulated savings. She might also have supported him other ways. He never said where the money came from. We lived frugally, but comfortably.

The question was, was he hanging onto a student just for the money?

"I've asked myself that a million times," he once said. "I've told her all I really know is sitting. I have nothing to give but that, and even that *I* don't give. Sitting does. There's no wisdom beyond the banal platitudes everyone knows.

"Madeleine says she gets something out of this, the talks I give. Interviews. Other casual encounters."

He came to Cambridge on a regular basis.

"I have to assume I'm doing something."

He was hardly aware of what he did with that listening, it came so natural to him. But it was rare, and priceless.

If there was one thing I hoped to learn from him, that was it.

Madeleine lived on Hampshire, one of those massive houses that have mostly been converted into businesses or apartments. The outside was already set up for the meditation center she'd been planning, with a high wooden fence around the grounds, a modest Zen garden with slabs of slate surrounded by small stones, a small pond with some carp, garden beds with a few plants.

There was a vestibule with a bell, and she met us at the door, wrapping Jake in a hug and kissing his mouth, actually hugging and kissing me, which was a first, at least for the past nineteen years. She led us into the house, bright and airy, not musty as I might have expected. Right at the entrance was a wide hall and a stairway to the second floor.

"How are you both?" she said. "Staying at that awful Y. I don't see why you don't stay here."

"It's not so bad," Jake said. "Hank likes to swim."

True enough. I hadn't been swimming yet, of course. Hadn't actually considered it.

"I could find Hank a place to swim," she said. "For heaven's sake."

She could build me a pool if she wanted.

"Can't you help me with this, Henry?" she said. Only she, in all the world, still called me that. She took Jake's arm. "He never lets me take care of him."

Jake was smiling, and they made a cute couple—though she was an inch taller, a quarter-century younger—but I could see, right at that moment, that Jake lost it. There was a certain *who is this woman and why is she holding onto me?* look to him. It wasn't fear, just bewilderment. He had that way of noticing, calming, then waiting, waiting.

"The man never wants much luxury," I said. "You should see where we ate breakfast."

"Not that Chinese donut house. Can you see me in there?"

Actually, Madeleine, no.

"I made the dreadful error of ordering sausage. My tummy's never been the same."

Jake was still in lala land. I wasn't worried. He was in the hands of the person who loved him most in the world. But my heart ached.

"Let me show you both what I've done to the place. Hank won't have much point of reference. We're about halfway to where we should be."

Madeleine, just a few years younger than I—in her early fifties—was still stunning. She was petite, though slightly taller than our little friar—with silvery hair that was right on the edge of blond, still bright and beautiful. She had kept her figure—no children, despite all the husbands—and had the high cheekbones, little bud of a mouth, that I associate with movie stars from the thirties. A single mole on the right cheek. She had the warmth and grace of a true aristocrat. Whatever her personal problems, she was brilliant with people.

"I bought this house with husband number two," she said. "Number two describes him rather well, I'm afraid. He was before your time, Henry, I believe."

"So was number three."

"Oh dear, really? The years do fly by, don't they?"

So do the husbands.

She had opened the door to one side of the hall and let us in. "This used to be the living room. I picture it as the zendo."

It had been entirely cleared out. The hardwood floors were newly refinished, bright and beautiful, lined with rows of *zabutons*—mats for meditation—and *zafus*, the round cushions. At the front of the room was an altar with a large Buddha, candles on either side of it, containers for holding incense. A far more elaborate setup than we had in Maine.

"My God," I said. "This is beautiful."

"What do you think, sweetheart?"

"Very nice." Jake nodded.

Madeleine finally noticed. She wasn't oblivious, just addressing her remarks to me, leading Jake by the arm. Now she heard that vague empty answer, turned to him, and looked.

"Are you all right, darling?" she said.

"Fine," he said, just barely there.

Madeleine could handle any social situation, but not any emotional one. Her face, which had worn a radiant smile, went to pieces.

"You are?" she said.

"This used to be the living room," I said. I took Jake's other arm. "Madeleine's house. Your favorite student."

"Hardly that," Madeleine said.

"The one who's been with you the longest," I said. "The one who's most loyal."

Suddenly, saying that, I knew it was true. It didn't matter how much she could or couldn't sit, had or hadn't done it. No one was more devoted to Jake. No one loved him more.

"This was the living room," I said. "What was it like?"

"Well." Madeleine's voice was halting. "There was a sofa right here." She pointed in front of us. "Another one there." She gestured to the end of the room, toward the street. "Lamps on either side. Sheer draperies coming down alongside the windows. Various chairs around. A piano in the corner."

"I remember," Jake said.

It wasn't what he said, but the way he said it. His voice didn't have that lost quality. He was back.

"This is amazing," he said. "I can't believe what you've done."

"I told you I was going to."

"I know. But actually seeing it."

Madeleine had regained her composure. She wasn't quite back to Jacqueline Kennedy Shows You the White House. But she was okay.

"The classroom is downstairs," she said. "That's the room

that needed the most work. I had to put in the flooring, repaint the walls. It's a large room, a little dark, maybe a little cool."

"Perfect for sitting," I said.

"I've imagined an office upstairs. Bedrooms for the two of you. There's a guest room as well. There could be another resident. And over time, if all this grows, there's a third floor as well. That could be a lecture hall, an alternate sitting room."

We were standing in a small triangle at that point, she talking about her dream, which was way beyond anything I'd heard, Jake completely back with us, listening and beaming. She started to cry.

She wasn't sobbing. She didn't break down. But tears just flowed from her eyes, ran down her cheeks.

"I've dreamed of this for so long," she said.

"It isn't that," Jake said. "It's that you hadn't seen this before. Me."

"It's all right."

"I've described it to her," he said to me. "But she hasn't seen it. She didn't believe it."

"I believed it."

"You hadn't seen it."

She had taken out a handkerchief, was wiping her eyes.

"Why don't you give us a minute, Hank?" Jake said. "You could take a look at the classroom."

"I'm all right, really," Madeleine said.

"I could sit," I said. "It never hurts."

"Do that," Jake said. "I'll come and get you."

The classroom was beautiful, cushions set out in rows. I sat for quite some time.

22

4

"SO WE'VE GOT TO FACE THIS NOW," Jake said. "We're all agreed?"

He, the focus of the situation, was the calmest person in the room. Madeleine, pouring tea—we sat at a table in the kitchen—avoided our eyes. She still seemed upset.

"It's a fact of nature," Jake said. "When you die, you give up everything you are. Your name, identity, your precious ideas. You're not a teacher anymore. Not a Buddhist. Not anything."

"Do we want some cookies with our tea?" Madeleine still hadn't raised her eyes.

"Why not?" Jake said.

Do you have to give up cookies when you die? *That* would be upsetting.

Madeleine got a tin of cookies from the counter, opened and put them in front of us, still not looking up. Her eyes were sad, her face somber.

"If you get old," Jake said, "if you're lucky enough to do that, you feel things going in your body, disappearing never to return. You've probably felt that. Both of you."

"Sure," I said.

"Sometimes it's the mind. The whole thing's unpredictable. It's all one process."

"Why are we talking about dying?" Madeleine said.

"It's all about dying," Jake said. "This whole practice. Letting go of all we are. What a relief."

One thing the man wasn't letting go of was that cookie. Nor was he so involved in what he said that he didn't appreciate it. He took a second bite. "Delicious."

"Darcy makes them," Madeleine said. "I agree."

She pushed the tin in my direction.

"I'm going to die," he said. "Probably soon."

The last lesson your teacher gives you is his death. The most valuable one.

"Please, darling." Madeleine's mouth trembled. "Don't say that." She covered his hand with hers.

"My heart's been a ticking time bomb for years," he said.

"And will be for years to come," I said.

"That's where you're not being realistic."

Especially if he kept slamming those cookies. He had taken another.

"If you create this center," he said, "it's going to be Hank who runs it."

She looked further down. She hadn't so much as sipped her tea.

And I hadn't considered running a center. I didn't know if I wanted to.

"I want that," Jake said. "That would be a good thing."

Madeleine looked up now. Her face had settled, eyes calmed.

"Nothing against Henry, of course," she said. "I'm sure he would run a wonderful center. But it's been my dream for years that you would come down here and teach. Make yourself more accessible. Be closer to me. That was selfish, of course. I wasn't thinking of it as simply starting a center."

"Nor was I," I said. "I must say."

"I've never actually heard Henry teach," she said.

There was a reason for that. I'd never taught.

"I'm sure he's a very good teacher," she said.

Only one doubter was left in the room. The man himself.

"Hank is my teaching," Jake said. "He embodies it."

"Jake," I said, "That's ridiculous."

"He's lived with me over twenty years. Heard every lecture I've given in that time."

"Hearing isn't living it." I looked straight at Madeleine. "I don't embody anything."

"If anyone in this world can carry on what I've done, it's him."

I didn't know what had come over him. If there was any real indication of senility, this was it. He had always emphasized that practice was the important thing, not his teaching, not anyone's. The dharma isn't rocket science. Most people got the gist after a while. The point isn't to know it. It's to live it.

"That's a ringing endorsement," Madeleine said. "It does make me feel better."

Unfortunately, it was based on nothing I'd ever done.

"The problem is that I knew Henry back when," Madeleine said. "That's not his fault. It's hard for me to make the transition."

"Hank's practiced for twenty-two years," Jake said.

To what effect? I sometimes wondered.

"It's hard to believe it's been that long," Madeleine said.

I wondered how she meant that.

The real problem was that she and I had some history together.

Back when I first met Jake, it had taken me a while to decide about practice. He had shown me about sitting, taught me some of the basics. For a year I tried by myself, sitting on my own, calling on the phone from time to time. But I've never been one for phone conversation, and there's something about the physical presence of the teacher. Teaching gets passed through the air. You've got to bang heads a little.

The main thing was that my life wasn't working out. I needed a drastic change, and I decided to go study with him.

I hadn't thought I'd stay. I figured one year of intense practice would give me a firm foundation. I could move to a new place, get a new job, make a new start.

Here I was twenty-some years later, still running a cash register.

In those days, most of Jake's teaching was in the summer. Some students stayed for considerable periods, Madeleine all summer. A class met twice a week, a sitting group every morning. I found a place to live and threw myself into it completely.

I suppose Madeleine was on the rebound from number three at that point. Maybe they were still married. Wouldn't have bothered me. She was beautiful, sophisticated, and rich, though I didn't know the extent of the money. She was vulnerable about relationships, quite vulnerable as a human being, though I didn't know how far that went. She worshipped Jake's teaching, clinging to it like a raft. It gave us something to talk about.

All that didn't matter, in a way. She could have been fat, ugly, poor, never heard a word about Jake: we still would have found each other. The Woman Who Can't Hold Onto a Man always finds The Man Who Adores Women, All Women. They fall into their dance effortlessly, as if they've done it dozens of times (in our case, we had). The only surprising thing was that we didn't get married.

I suppose what saved us was the tourist season; it played out quickly, like a shipboard romance. Maybe meditation had something to do with that. We had hardly gotten to know each other before we realized we'd known each other all our lives. Not *you* again! It was so brief that there weren't a lot of hard feelings. Just the humiliation of doing it *again*.

26

I could understand how Madeleine had trouble seeing me as a teacher. She was quite gracious under the circumstances.

"What we plan to do," Jake said, sipping—perhaps slurping (there was a little of the cab driver still in him)—his tea, "is co-teach this retreat." He glanced at the cookie tin.

"All right."

"We'll sit up front together, and I'll start. Won't make a big deal out of the fact that Hank's there. But if I start to falter, or completely lose it, he'll take over."

"That sounds difficult." Madeleine glanced at me.

You said it, sister.

"It's the only way I can do it," Jake said.

"I just hope you won't be defeatist," she said. "There's no reason to assume something will go wrong."

"It's true," I said. "You're coherent around me for hours at a time."

"I'm faking some of that. I have lots of little lapses."

"You can talk through those," Madeleine said.

I was with her. I'd be happy to sit there and look pretty. Enigmatic. Whatever.

"We'll see," Jake said. "God willing, I'll continue."

I hoped he wouldn't reference God in a Buddhist talk.

"And I hope you won't give up on running the center," Madeleine said. "That's still my deepest dream. That your spirit will inform it."

"It will," he said. "One way or another."

Who knows what he meant by that? Maybe this was one of those lapses.

You couldn't tell the lapses from the wisdom.

He still eyed the cookie tin. If he resists this temptation, I thought, if he can have the willpower to slow down a little, everything's going to be fine. He'll give the talks. I'll sit there, just like the old days. I made a little bet with myself.

"We've got to get going," Jake said. "Hank's got a luncheon date." He reached into the tin and took two cookies.

Christ.

He seemed to reconsider for a moment, then took a third.

"Luncheon date," Madeleine said. *"Cherchez la femme."*

They never forget, do they?

"It's my son," I said. "He works up here."

"That's right."

"He's quite the young man," Jake said.

Not so young, actually.

"I wish I'd known this," Madeleine said, taking Jake's arm on our way out. "I would have cancelled my appointment."

"I'll come tomorrow. I'm headed for that goofball bookstore."

"You'll be all right, by yourself?"

"I can go stark raving mad in there and they'll never notice."

"That's enough talk about going crazy," Madeleine said. "And about dying. You don't have to teach all the time."

That was Jake's flaw, if he had one. He couldn't turn it off.

"We want you with us forever," she said.

"I will be," he said. "You can count on it."

Now what was he talking about?

5

THE GOOFBALL SPIRITUAL BOOKSTORE in question used to be at Harvard Square but was now on Mass. Ave. near Central. Jake loved the place. Apparently no one had told the owner there was such a thing as returns, so he had a huge back stock on Buddhism and Zen. He also had major sections on Edgar Cayce, Madame Blavatsky, UFOs, astrology. Boldly displayed at the front for years was a Benjamin Franklin compilation entitled *Fart Proudly*. He gave as much space to total quacks as to renowned teachers.

"That's as it should be," Jake said. "How do we know who's right?"

Jake combed the Buddhist section but ranged far and wide, might spend long afternoons leafing through some obscure Indian sage. He also loved talking to the guy who ran the place, a Carlos Castaneda freak who loved to bullshit.

We took our time walking down. I wasn't meeting Josh until one.

"Why did you say that stuff?" I asked. "That I'm your dharma heir."

"I don't know who is, if not you. Do I have one?"

The old man was trudging along, taking in the morning air, beaming in the sun, munching his cookies.

"I came to you all screwed up," I said. "Stayed because I needed time. More than other people."

"Everybody starts because they're screwed up. That's why the Buddha started. Dogen was a homeless orphan."

So was Kodo Sawaki, the man who taught Jake's teacher.

"I stayed because I couldn't leave," I said.

"Maybe the first year or two. After that you wanted to go deeper. The old life wouldn't satisfy you."

The old life looked pallid beside what I did with Jake, much as I liked some of it.

"I wouldn't have let you just hang on," he said.

In the Buddha's day, too, many people decided to stay. They preferred the new life they'd found, difficult as it was.

"I talked to Madeleine the way I had to, so she'd understand. It's not the way I usually put things. But it's not a lie."

If he meant all that, it was humbling. It was scary.

"I screwed this up, bringing you along as a teacher," he said. "I didn't have a model. I've waited too long."

"I thought your Japanese teacher was your model."

"Those guys were so eccentric, for the twentieth century. And Buddhism was ancient in that culture. It's not the same here."

Jake had done his real training in Japan. Nothing else seemed quite right after that. He wound up in Maine, as far from California as he could get.

"I should have brought you along more slowly," he said, "had you giving talks. Splitting them, at least."

"Your students didn't want that."

"Who cares what they wanted? It's a matter of what they need. Now there's no time."

We'd made it to Harvard Street, one of my favorites in all of Cambridge, shady and peaceful, big houses on a little hill back from the street. The leaves were just starting to turn.

"You want this last cookie?" Jake said.

"You're offering me your last cookie?" Greater love hath no man.

"I thought you needed one. You didn't take any." Incomprehensible to Jake.

"I'm fine, really."

He popped it into his mouth.

"You'll have to develop on your own," he said after a while. "But you have a teaching sense. You started that way."

High school social studies, years ago.

"And don't underestimate Madeleine. Even the Buddha had wealthy patrons. Buddhism would be nowhere in this country if people hadn't paid the bills."

"Is she your girlfriend?"

The question just popped out on me. It had been percolating since we'd left.

He burst into laughter. "At my age?"

"Was she ever?"

He heaved a big sigh.

"I've always wondered," I said.

He shrugged. "How much time do we have?"

"Twenty minutes."

"Let's walk down here."

He liked the shady sidewalks of Harvard Street too.

"When you do this kind of work, you're getting to a deep place in people. Every human being's got it, even the ones who don't last in practice. They just can't face it."

"Right."

"It's the same in various endeavors. Art school. Writing. Probably politics, some way I don't get. People get engaged with that deep energy. Spiritual. Sexual. It's all the same down there."

"I don't know about politics."

"Maybe not. But people confuse the teaching with the teacher. Think you're wonderful because you give them a glimpse of the dharma. What's wonderful is the dharma."

"Yes."

"The women all think they want in your pants. That's what it comes down to."

Maybe I did want to be a teacher.

"A doddering old man with heart problems and Alzheimer's. It's ridiculous."

"You don't have Alzheimer's."

"I don't know what the hell you'd call it. That is the name, isn't it?"

"Yeah."

"I thought I forgot even that." He shook his head. "Anyway, some guys take advantage of this. You've heard the stories."

"Sure."

"I'm not telling you what to do. You can be one of them. You've got a history with this."

I did.

"And it ruins the whole thing. You become the boyfriend and the teacher flies out the window."

Maybe I should take up cookies.

"Those guys all did it, of course," I said. "The ones in the stories."

"They were kidding themselves if they thought they were teaching."

He had never made that statement so strongly. It sounded like his last word on the subject.

"I'm not saying don't have sex. Just don't mix it with teaching."

We had made it to Prospect and were walking to Mass. Ave., cars all jammed up, fighting to get around each other. The peaceful stretch of our walk was over.

"I never touched Madeleine," he said. "She's been all over

me as long as I've known her. It's important to her, that lovey-dovey stuff. Doesn't matter how much money the woman has. Emotionally, she's a street person."

We had made it to the corner of Mass. Ave., speaking of street people. He was going one way, I the other.

"I don't think I put up with it for the money," he said. "I've wondered."

"You didn't."

He'd have done the same for a suicidal poor person.

"I've turned down more than I've taken."

I did wonder how much he'd taken. The money lecture was for another time.

"Are you going to be all right," I asked, "alone?"

"We've got a two-block radius here."

The Y was almost in front of the bookstore. Plenty of restaurants around.

"If I disappear, check the bakeries first."

He would never take this seriously.

"If you never touched Madeleine," I said, "how do you know all this?"

"There was somebody I did touch. I've been wanting to tell you. If there's time."

"We've had twenty-two years."

"It hasn't been right until now." An enigmatic statement if there ever was one. "Probably I'll survive the afternoon. Say hello to the boy."

He was a man. Nearly middle-aged. "I will. Take care of yourself."

The old man was just joking, but every time I left, I wondered if it was the last time.

I could have taken the subway into Boston, had done it plenty of times, but I preferred to walk, past MIT and over the bridge into town. It was exhilarating walking over the water, the wind blowing like crazy; you saw joggers, rollerbladers, bikers, old guys getting out, students trudging under back-packs, old ladies with shopping bags. The whole world came at you over that bridge.

Every one of them a Buddha, according to the teaching. Ponder *that*.

Josh's passionate interests, as with few people I knew, had turned into a career. He had always liked movies—what kid didn't?—and his early years were fruitful: *Star Wars* alone was a major obsession. When his mother and I split up, he was twelve; he stayed with me on Sundays, and the one thing we did every week was go to a movie.

Partly I just didn't know what else to do, suddenly a single parent; partly it had always been our favorite thing, and his mother never approved, thinking we should be out walking the Appalachian Trail or something; partly it was just that the Sunday second matinee was a great time to go. We ate dinner out afterward, talked about what we'd seen. It was my favorite moment in the week.

The occasion became legendary among our friends. "What's the movie today?" they said if they saw us in the morning. Sometimes they asked to come, but a certain kind of critical mind didn't make it. Josh was the only human being I'd ever known who shared my rock-bottom conviction: any movie was better than no movie. We were sometimes disappointed, but never sorry we'd gone. After a real dog we'd come out laughing.

Siskel and Ebert were syndicated on Sunday evening, and we watched that too. Josh began keeping a log, which he typed up and gave to friends. When I moved to Mount Desert he came for the summer, and there was a theater in Bar Harbor that showed a different movie every night. A couple of summers we went to every single one. We went late the nights of my class with Jake. The same movie showed on Saturdays and Sundays, and sometimes we went twice. It was disgraceful.

But now he was one of the best known reviewers in the country. The *Globe* gave him space, and he could use it any way he wanted, give the whole column to one movie, split it up among five. He wrote in a wild idiomatic style that I, for one, found superb. He had the same love for movies he'd had when he was twelve.

Josh picked the kind of restaurant I never go to, one of those big city places, high ceilings full of the roar of conversation and clatter of plates, white cloths on the tables and good silverware, waiters dashing around with big trays. Deals were closing all over the room. He was waiting for me when I got there, or so the hostess said; it was like picking my way through a maze, finding the table.

But he looked great. He's six feet, two inches tall, half a foot taller than I am—his mother is tall—and though he started as a skinny, gawky kid, he's filled out as he's gotten older. He also has his mother's reddish hair; his is curly, and he lets it grow into a near-Afro, quite distinctive. He wears pale-framed glasses, always dresses well, today in a light sport jacket, starched shirt, jeans. The man has style. He stood to hug me in that booming, bustling restaurant. It's always great to see him.

Especially when we're seated, he towers over me.

"You walked down?" he asked.

"I did. Our old walk." In the old days, when we went to Mount Desert, we would stay in Cambridge a few days and often took that walk.

"Is this," he asked, "as my friends would say, a 'woman's lunch,' or a man's?"

"What's a 'woman's lunch'?"

"We have wine. A glass of Chardonnay. Men have a drink."

"Does beer qualify?"

"You're a man. We'll call you a man."

He had a bourbon and water, small glass. I had a Sam Adams. We were in Boston.

We gave some attention to the menu. Stiff prices at this place. I was glad it was his turn.

"Going to the movies today?" I asked. What a question. When didn't he?

"One of those kid flicks. Some kid's acting weird, turns out he has special powers. He can see the dead, talk to the devil, some fucking thing. Pretty soon his parents are swelling up like bullfrogs, the house is imploding. I've seen it a million times. The bane of my existence."

"Any movie is better than no movie."

"We may have to alter that principle, honest to God." He closed his menu. "You could come."

"I have to watch the old man. I'll take a rain check."

"How is he?"

"Not great. Hard to tell, actually. He hides it. Cheerful as ever."

Josh had come up a couple of times during the summer, noticed Jake's absent air around the shop.

"He could fall into a shit heap and smell like roses," I said. I'd never seen anything like it.

"I just realized the other day," I said, "I'm the age he was when I met him."

"He looked older."

"Bald guys do. You're the age I was."

"Holy shit. It's scary."

Our drinks arrived and we ordered. Lamb chops for him—ah to be young—a salad and crab cake appetizer for me. Maybe this *was* a woman's lunch.

"How's Carol?" I said.

"It's Mitzi, Dad. Carol was before."

"Jesus, that's right. Maybe I'm the one with Alzheimer's. How's Mitzi?"

It was hard to keep them straight.

"So so. You know how it goes."

If the biggest influence on a man's life is the unlived life of his father—it makes sense when you think of it—Josh was living the life I'd always wanted, or thought I did. One woman after another. No thought of marrying. Several had moved in for a while, never too long. They kept getting younger. At least in comparison to him.

I was married right out of college, Josh born right away. I wanted that too, of course, and it was partly just the time, war raging all around us, me looking for a little stability. It was a different choice.

Josh had always seemed confident in his.

He took up his drink. "Something's wrong," he said.

"With Mitzi?"

"No. Mitzi's okay. She's just Mitzi." He looked into his glass, sipped. "Mitzi's not going to last."

I could have told him that. If I'd remembered her name.

"It's just something wrong. Not a catastrophe. Not dire. It's vague. Like what I just said about that movie. It's a bad season. Or I'm not writing well."

"I read you every week. Seems fine."

"Have you seen the blog?"

"Sometimes. It's not like the reviews. Blogs aren't the same." One thing I didn't understand about this generation was why they published every word they wrote. We kept journals and left them in a drawer. People lived their lives so publicly these days.

I was the man's father, of course, but I'd have said if I thought he was slipping.

"That's what's so weird," he said. "The movie season really isn't worse. I seem to write as well as ever, though it takes longer. Mitzi's like the other girls. Better than a lot."

He killed his drink. Our lunch was arriving.

"But something's wrong," he said.

The waiter served. We declined second drinks. I was having both of my dishes together. Josh began to pick at his.

It was crashingly obvious what was wrong. I just didn't know how to say it.

"Roger Ebert," he said. "How does he do it? All these years later."

"I wonder if he does."

"Still seems good to me."

The eternal human question. How will this all turn out? How will it be when I'm . . . whatever. It always makes us unhappy. And we always ask it. That's what the Buddha noticed. We can't let the moment be.

The problem was that I couldn't help him. A father is a model—often of what not to do—but can't be a mentor. He has to stand by helplessly, hoping someone will step in.

"You're at that time of life," I said. "Lost in a dark wood. Read Dante."

"I saw the movie."

"They made a movie of that?"

"It's a joke, Dad. Around the office."

I get it. Movie critic jokes.

"It's not a bad thing," I said. "You're in a dark wood. Stay there a while."

"It doesn't feel good."

"No." And a father hates to see his son suffer. The Buddha's father was a case in point. "But it's a mistake to get out too fast. To fake it."

That's what everybody does. Runs out of the cave before they find the mystery. The cave's their one chance.

"Are you seeing a shrink?" I asked.

"I've been thinking about it. Mitzi says I should." He shrugged. "So I'll decide to marry her."

I wished I could remember what Mitzi looked like. I think I was picturing Carol.

"I think you should too," I said.

He looked up.

"See somebody, that is. Mitzi's right. Somebody older." While you're at it, find somebody older than Mitzi.

"You've got to figure out what the next thing is," I said. "There is a next thing. You've got to find it. But you don't want to grab too fast. You let it emerge." I had to shut my mouth. I'd already said too much. What I suspected—but would never have said—was that he needed to write a screenplay. Talk about the scary unknown. California here I come.

"I won't mention what I did at your age."

"Jesus. I hope it's not that."

"It's not. I'm sure." You never do what your father did.

"I'm worried about you," he said. "That's part of it."

"Don't be," I said.

"How can I not? What's going to happen?"

That question again. What must he have imagined, his old derelict Zen monk father moving in, sleeping on a mat in the corner, waking every morning to chant and do prostrations, shaving his head weekly, living on rice and pickled radishes, walking the city streets with a begging bowl?

I told him about the center, told him the way Madeleine had fixed up the house, the bedrooms upstairs, the future office, plans for the third floor. I said these things despite the fact that I hadn't known about them four hours before. Also despite the fact that—in my best guess—they required Jake's sane presence on the earth for at least another eight or nine months. They also required his moving from Maine, something I couldn't quite picture. There were lots of ifs.

"What if Jake doesn't make it?" Josh saw one of them.

"He wants me to do it anyway."

"Do you want that?"

Good question. This was all so sudden. I knew how Josh felt when he sat down with Mitzi.

"I'm deciding," I said.

It was another of those moments when you sit in the cave.

6

I MET JAKE the summer Josh and I first went to Mount Desert Island. Josh's mother and I had separated the winter before, and it was important that we go on vacation, but I thought it would be unbearable to go to the North Carolina beaches we'd always gone to. We'd do the same old things, be constantly reminded of the person who wasn't there. We were still wounded and shaky.

A New York friend of mine named Cheryl owned a small house on Mount Desert Island and rented it out during the tourist season; she thought it a perfect place for a new vacation. The ocean up there was too cold for swimming in June, but there were beautiful lakes for canoeing, a miniature golf course and a go-cart track, a beautiful national park for hiking and biking; the town of Bar Harbor was full of superb restaurants and quaint shops. Cheryl herself went up there every summer with whoever her current boyfriend was. She always had a wonderful time.

The first mistake I made—in a summer that would be full of them—was thinking of New England as a small enclave; we'd fly into Boston and drive up to Mount Desert, no problem. Actually it's quite a distance—as any fool who looks at a map can tell—and a travel agent put us on a puddle jumper to Portland, had us rent a car there. We still had a decent drive ahead of us, and it was late and pitch black when we got to the island. We were picking up the key from somebody's mailbox, finding the house with directions that were perfect in daylight but a little tricky at night. I'm talking no streetlights, most of the houses closed and dark. I wasn't sure I had the right place until the key fit.

What a relief, after an endless day of travel, finally to have found our house. We could relax.

Except that there was nothing to do.

I had heard Cheryl describe long blessed days of quiet and solitude in her Mount Desert cottage. She once sent a list of the fifteen books she had read during a two-week vacation. She spoke of a protected back porch where she could sunbathe nude, long afternoons of marvelous sex with the current boyfriend, evenings with wine and a lobster from a lobster shack. She did mention that there was no television or stereo in the house, just an AM radio. There wasn't even a phone. I hadn't taken all that in.

Josh at that time was the aforementioned tall gawky kid, twelve years old but looked fourteen or fifteen, all legs and arms, the wild red hair. He wasn't a TV addict, but definitely liked it, would have used it to settle into any other place we'd gone. He liked to read—had a huge collection of comics—but not *all day*. He'd never eaten a lobster. Neither had I, actually. He sure as hell wasn't interested in sunbathing nude. He wanted to *do* things, was full of jittery nervous energy.

We'd made this apparently endless trip to paradise, and there not only wasn't cable, there wasn't anything. The top forty on the radio.

We kept wandering around the cottage, looking for something. What I really needed was a stiff drink—Josh too, probably—but there wasn't any booze. We settled down for the evening, Josh on a daybed out in the living room, me in the bedroom where Cheryl spent her glorious afternoons.

I was starting to realize—perhaps hadn't quite started—how much I was counting on that vacation to make amends. I'd totally fucked up my marriage—that was the way I felt at that point—put Josh through all kinds of hell (I'd been a basket case all winter, searching around frantically for another woman), but now I would emerge, after a brief slump (happens to even a superstar) as a great father. I was going to bypass the boring vacations from the past (which we had always loved) and take us to a famous resort, show Josh the time of his life.

Suddenly it looked like a complete disaster.

I don't know how to describe what happened to me that night. At the time it seemed totally out of left field, one of the strangest things I ever went through. Now it seems the obvious consequence of all I'd experienced over the past eight months. It did concentrate a great deal of emotional reaction into one night, but it had to; I hadn't slowed down enough before that.

I'd been reading in bed and turned off the light—Josh had turned his off a few minutes before—when a tremendous anxiety rush came over me. It was very much physical—my heart started to pound, palms to sweat, my body simultaneously to flush and go cold, tremble. A doctor would probably have called it a panic attack. That was strange enough. But what was really strange were the thoughts that—at incredible speed—began to run through my head.

What if something happened to me that night? What if I had a heart attack and died (the symptoms I felt at that moment seemed very much like a heart attack)? What would Josh do? My own father had died when I was a teenager, and I'd always feared putting Josh through that trauma, but the circumstances that night were especially horrific. We were in a remote place we knew nothing about; there was no phone; most of the houses around were unoccupied. What would he do in that house with a dead father?

What if—this seemed even worse—I had a heart attack but was not yet dead, he had to go out on that dark gravel road and find help? We didn't know anybody. We were in a state famous for being inhospitable. What if he went banging on doors and was greeted only by wizened old guys with shotguns who told him to go away, or took a shot at him?

What if—my mind was racing—*I* did something to him? What if I went crazy and attacked him because he wasn't wild about the vacation I'd taken so much trouble to put together? I was angry at his reaction so far, I had to admit (though it was exactly like my own). What if I beat him, tried to kill him? These thoughts seemed insane—I'd never laid a hand on my son—but insane was what I seemed to be at that moment, and you read such things in the paper every day. What if he fought me off and killed me? What would that be like to live with? How would he explain it to the police (if he could ever find any)?

These thoughts took all of about ten seconds to run through my head, and were nothing compared to the images that accompanied them. They proliferated endlessly: I couldn't believe what I was seeing, couldn't stop it.

I look back on the young man I was, younger than Josh was now (Dante thought *he* went through hell at midlife), and see someone facing a huge load of stress, literally bursting with it, with no idea how to handle it. The images his mind saw were extreme, but they had been trying to get his attention for eight months (while he was trying to get laid). He was facing fear, the same fear we all face, the fear that Josh was feeling right now: What is going to become of me, and those I love? His mind just created some unusual possibilities.

Craving, aversion, and delusion, as the Buddha pointed out. This was aversion, big time. Or maybe delusion. Who gives a shit?

The images went on for hours. One of the worst things was that I had no one to talk to. I certainly couldn't talk to Josh.

("Son, I've been thinking about killing you.") It was a dreadful night, not the greatest start to a vacation.

One of the problematic aspects of that cottage for us (again, Cheryl loved its remoteness) was that you had to get in a car to do anything at all. In North Carolina the beach was right out the door, the fishing pier a hundred yards away.

The vaunted miniature golf course wasn't as good as the one in North Carolina. The go-cart track was fun, but after a half-hour (the minimum) you'd had enough for the summer (if not for the rest of your life).

The morning we went out in a canoe—had to do something, bored out of our minds—was too windy, and we had trouble getting around. Josh actually had more experience in canoes than I, kept telling me how to maneuver. We almost went over a couple of times. We finally made it back to the dock a half hour late, had to pay for an extra half-day.

We drove the car around the national park, and it was breathtaking; I kept exclaiming at it. Josh glanced out the window now and then. Finally he said, in one of the memorable quotes from the summer, "Dad, I've had about all the beauty I can take."

The movie theater with its nightly changes was our saving grace, but that only killed a couple of hours. (A couple of times I almost said, "Want to go in and watch it again?") The restaurants were great, and we were good at eating, though our foray into the world of lobsters was a total failure. A diagram came with the dinner—"What kind of dinner comes with a diagram?" Josh said. "What is it, a model airplane?"—but we had a huge amount of trouble dismembering the creature and finding the meat. It was one of those dinners where you worked so hard that you were hungry again when you finished. "I don't actually *like* this dish all that much," Josh said, an opinion with which I concurred. "Why don't these people just drink a cup of butter?"

The nights weren't going too well after that first shaky one. I closed my eyes expecting to see those visions, and did, but not as intensely as at first. I was sleeping about half of what I usually did.

On the fourth day, we went to do the one thing we hadn't tried. Rent bikes.

The thing I will always remember about Jake, the first time we saw him, was that he took one look at Josh and beamed all over. This was a kid whose legs and arms were utterly unpredictable, whose face was spotted with freckles and the beginnings of acne—he was way ahead of himself—whose hair looked like an unmade bed, but Jake saw him as a perfect specimen of humanity, as if Jesus Christ had walked in to rent a bike. He didn't treat him like a kid, spoke to us like a couple of men.

"What are you guys up to?" he asked. He sat behind the counter eating lunch, a pasta salad.

"Renting bikes, I guess," Josh said. "That's what *he* says." He jerked a thumb at me.

"Sounds good to me," Jake said.

"We thought we'd try a couple of the dirt bikes," I said. "Josh has been wanting to."

"Of course he has," Jake said.

"Take them up and ride through the park."

"Sounds very good to me."

That became *the* most memorable quotation of the summer. Jake used it for almost everything we said. We spent the whole next year using it ourselves, in all kinds of circumstances.

From the back another guy came out, a short, wiry, dark man, dressed in a cycling get-up. "I'll take care of them, Jake," he said. "You're eating."

"I can eat any time."

"It's okay. I'm free. I got it."

Josh and Jake were looking at each other, Jake grinning all over, as if at some huge joke.

"Sounds very good to me," he said.

The young man, who turned out to be one of the owners, took us out and got us set up. He was extremely efficient, and the bikes were beautiful, brand new. He got a map, sketched out a route to the park. He actually walked us over and pointed at the road where the route began. These weren't canoes, and it wasn't windy. I saw no way this could go wrong.

Five minutes later we were peddling up an extraordinarily steep hill, trying to shift into lower and lower gears, cars whizzing all around.

I should have noticed—it was right there in front of me—that the owner was an incredible bike jock, had legs of steel, and even he said it was "a little steep at first." Josh had started off in front, wildly enthusiastic, but now was wobbling all over the place, trying hard to shift. My legs were stronger; I was gaining on him.

"This is no good," he said. "Are you sure this is the road?"

"Of course it's the road. He pointed to it. The park's up ahead. We've just got to ride."

"I can't fucking ride." He got off and started to walk.

"Don't walk out here. It's dangerous. Shift to a lower gear."

"I *can't.*"

"I thought you knew how to ride these things."

"I said I *wanted* to know."

"Just try it. This is your chance."

I rode past him. It was as if this were my last opportunity. If I couldn't make this day fun, the whole vacation was ruined. I was a failure as a father. He *had* to like it.

I had ridden another hundred yards when I noticed Josh had crossed the road and was heading back down.

It seemed to take forever to get across the road and ride

down after him. By the time I did he was almost to the bottom and wasn't stopping, pedaling like crazy. I couldn't let him out of my sight.

The bike shop was in what used to be a house, and Jake—having finished lunch—had come out on the porch. He stood with that beaming smile on his face. Josh rode right in front of him—I had picked up speed, was almost there—when Josh got off the bike, threw it down, and started to scream, picking it up and throwing it down again, picking it up and throwing it down.

"This is not my fucking bike, this is not my fucking trip, this is not my fucking vacation, this is not what I fucking wanted to do," on and on, delivering his opinion on nearly everything that had happened in the past four days, and finally got down to, "not my fucking divorce, not my fucking father, not my fucking fucked-up life." His face was roughly the color of his hair, and his voice almost screeched, tears pouring from his eyes.

The owner came out beside Jake and would have jumped down, but Jake put an arm out to stop him. I wouldn't say Jake's expression hadn't changed—he looked concerned—but he was definitely still smiling, that broad smile that never seemed to fade. Because he didn't do anything, I didn't either.

We all stood staring for a moment, waiting for the dust to settle.

"Other than that, how'd you like the bike?" Jake said.

"Not too fucking much. It wouldn't fucking shift."

I had not heard Josh use that particular word to such an extent. I'd hardly heard him use it at all.

"It probably won't fucking shift at *this* point," Jake said.

The owner, furious and perplexed, stared at Jake.

"You just stand there while he wrecks the bike?" he said.

"I can fix it," Jake said.

"Not if he's bent something. Not if it's bent beyond repair."

"I can fix it, Harold," Jake said. "Believe me."

"I'll pay for the damages," I said.

"You're damn straight," Harold said. "A damaged bike is *never* the same. You ought to pay for the bike."

Jake had stepped off the porch, picked the bike up from the ground, looked at it.

"Nothing's new forever," he said. He was looking at the pedal and gears, trying to turn them. "Why did you send them up that hill, Harold?"

"It's the best ride," Harold said. "The most scenic entrance to the park."

"*Scenic?*" Josh said, wiping his face.

"Once you get up the hill," Harold said. "It's the best way in. I *said* the hill was steep."

"It's not the best for someone on the bike for the first time," Jake said. "Who hasn't learned to shift down, gotten a little used to it."

"It's the route I recommend," Harold said. "The best way to the park."

"You might reconsider," Jake said. He was still fiddling with the bike. "I can fix this," he said.

"Good," Josh said. "I'm sorry. I didn't mean to do that."

I was rather shaken at that point, staring at my son.

"What exactly did you mean?" Harold asked.

"You boys had lunch?" Jake said, looking at Josh.

Josh shook his head.

"We were going to eat at that place in the park," I said. "The one with popovers."

"This place next door has good calzones," Jake said. "You hungry?" Still looking at Josh.

"Kind of," Josh said.

"Works up an appetite, doesn't it son?" Harold said. "Wrecking a bike."

That Harold was quite a wit.

"Let's go over there," Jake said. "Let's pretend this rental never happened."

"Never *happened?*" Harold said.

"I'm on my lunch hour," Jake said. "I'll be back."

I left my bike in front of the bewildered-looking Harold. I was somewhat bewildered myself. Josh and Jake walked ahead of me. They were roughly the same height, with rather different body shapes. The odd feeling, which I couldn't get over, was that they were old friends, rough contemporaries, this fifty-five-year-old round bald man and my gawky, awkward, wild-haired son. I was tagging along. Perfectly welcome, of course.

The other thing that struck me was that Jake seemed in charge. He seemed in charge of any situation he was in.

The pizza place had also once been a house, had a counter where you ordered and a large dining area in front of it, like an enclosed porch. The owners were apparently obsessed with the Grateful Dead, whose pictures lined the walls. The place was empty at that hour, a little before noon.

"You like Italian sausage?" Jake asked.

"Sure," Josh said.

"That's what I recommend. How about your old man?"

"I better have it plain." I wasn't the least bit hungry.

"Couple of Cokes?" Jake asked.

"I think I'll have a beer," I said.

"Good idea," Jake said.

We walked to a table with our drinks. Jake wasn't having anything.

He stuck out a hand as we sat down. "Jake Weinstein," he said.

"Henry Wilder," I said. "And Josh."

The two of them shook hands. We all sat down.

"You're on vacation?" Jake asked.

"Hasn't been the best trip of our lives," I said.

We told him about our late arrival, about the house, our trips to miniature golf and the go-cart track, our disaster with the lobsters, the outing on the lake.

"He doesn't know how to paddle," Josh said. "He's stronger, so he needs to be in back. But he can't do it."

"You can't teach him?" Jake asked.

"Not so far."

"Then you need to be in back."

It had actually been my first time in a canoe. Josh had used one at summer camp.

By that time our food had arrived. I'd been a little suspicious, what with the photos, but the calzones were great.

"This probably isn't the best time to ride to the park," Jake said. "There's a lot of traffic, a lot of people once you get there. That also wasn't the best way to send you. Nice entrance, but hard to get to."

"I'm sorry I fucked up the bike," Josh said.

What had happened to my son's vocabulary?

"I can fix it," Jake said. "Tomorrow's my day off. I take a ride in the morning. What do you say we meet at eight and I show you some things. A better entrance, some good trails to ride. How to shift gears."

"That might help," Josh said.

"Harold means well. He just doesn't understand."

"We appreciate this," I said. It was the first thing that had gone right that week.

"So I'll see you guys at eight."

"That is a little early," Josh said.

"That's when it happens," Jake said.

"All right."

"I'll see you guys in the morning," Jake said.

He got up to walk out, came back after a few steps.

"There's something around here called a lobster roll," he said. "Lots of places have it. They get the meat out and serve it on some kind of bun. It's overpriced, but avoids all the hassle. You don't need a diagram."

"I'll try it," Josh said.

Jake walked out. We both stared.

"I've never met anybody like that guy," Josh said.

"Me neither."

"Where does a guy like that come from?"

We had to get up at the crack of dawn after a late movie, but I didn't hear a word of complaint from Josh, who'd been complaining about everything. The town was deserted except for a diner down the street from the bike shop where all the locals gathered and blueberry pancakes flew off the griddle at a terrific rate.

Harold was behind the counter at the bike shop, looking worried. Jake took us on the street and rode us up and down, showed us about the gears.

"The whole thing is not waiting too long to downshift, especially on a hill. You don't want to do it too early, but if you wait too long you can't do it at all."

After that we went for a ride, following Jake. He took a back entrance to the park, not as nice as the one Harold suggested—which we did finally come to—but much more accessible. The park had roads for cars but also carriage paths that had been created years before by some Rockefeller and were perfect for dirt bikes, complicated to navigate, but Jake knew them inside and out.

The place was dead quiet at that hour, dew still on the grass. Twice we startled deer, and once Jake stopped and motioned for us to stop behind him. A deer stood in the woods not twenty feet away, staring at us. Finally it bounded away.

Jake didn't say a word after he showed us the gears. He didn't even say anything about the deer. He apparently thought the place spoke for itself. A couple of times when we were climbing steep hills he slowed down for us while we shifted; otherwise he set a wicked pace, didn't stop until we were back at the shop.

"You really know those paths," I said.

"I ride every day."

"Always at this hour?" Josh asked.

"Earlier. I was being easy on you guys."

"*Earlier?*" Josh would take a two-hour nap that afternoon.

"I get up at four," Jake said. "I like the morning."

Josh stood there with his mouth hanging open.

We didn't get up at four, but for the rest of that vacation took an early bike ride (and an afternoon nap). It became as much a fixture as the evening movie. We never did run into Jake. Must not have been early enough.

A couple of days later, while we were walking in town, Josh said another thing that improved the vacation.

"Do we always have to, you know, hang around together?"

"Meaning what?"

"I'm on vacation. I don't want to be with my father every minute. No offense."

I was slightly startled. He'd wanted to be with me in the past.

"At the beach I could go to the pier myself. Or take a walk."

"You want to be alone?"

"I just don't want to be with my *father* all the time. Every minute."

It was starting to sink in. It just hadn't occurred to me.

"You go that way," I said. "I'll go this. I'll meet you at the bike shop at five."

"Make it five thirty," Josh said. "And one more thing."

"Yeah?"

"I can't just walk around here with no money in my pocket."

I went to the bike shop right away. I'd been wanting to do that since that first afternoon. I wanted to go without Josh.

Jake sat behind the counter working on some gear. He

always seemed to do a job casually, never puzzled over it. He never seemed to be working.

"I wanted to thank you for what you did for us," I said. "I don't know how you managed that."

"I didn't do anything," he said.

"That's why it worked out. Anyone else would have."

He nodded, smiling. "It's easier when it's not your own son."

"This is you, isn't it?" I pointed to a flyer for a meditation group.

"It is."

"Where'd you learn?"

"Japan, mostly. I was there for years."

"I'm wondering if that could help me."

"It's been a great help to me. That's why I have the group."

"You just sit there? Chant something?"

"Come on Thursday. Come early, so I can show you."

"Josh and I go to the movie."

"Bring him along. Or let him go alone. He'd probably like some time by himself." Apparently the man was a mind reader.

Josh wanted to come, as it turned out. He liked being around Jake, even tried sitting, though his knobby legs were all over the place, twelve-year-old energy rumbling. He drew the line at staying for the group. Ten minutes were plenty for him. We actually made the second showing at the theater.

I could hardly believe something so simple—sitting cross-legged with a straight posture, gazing at the wall—was the secret to who Jake was. He showed us in a matter-of-fact way, the same way he'd explained shifting gears on the bikes. But I started to do it every morning, mostly because he inspired confidence, also because I was desperate, my life was so out of whack. Everything had come to a head when I took that vacation.

Though I wasn't having night fears anymore. They ended the night after Josh threw his fit.

I attended the group the next week; Josh went to the movie

alone. That was my first glimpse of Madeleine, though I don't actually remember.

The last day of vacation, we stopped by the bike shop to say good-bye. Jake had turned our whole summer around.

"I don't know that we'll ever be back," I said.

"Not to that hell hole." Josh had come to hate the house.

"There's a cheap motel at the end of the next street," Jake said. "Down by the water. Not fancy enough for the average tourist. No kitchenettes. But it does have cable, which might please some people."

"Now you're talking," Josh said.

"And you can take your breakfasts at the diner." That down-home place we'd gone the first day we rode bikes. "Calzone and pizza for lunch. The best part is that you don't have to drive. Rent bikes for the week. Freelance. You can hang around and read, the way you like." He nodded to me. "Josh can be out stalking girls."

"They stalk me, Jake." It was the first time I'd heard that. "I think it's the red hair. Drives them wild."

"Anyway," Jake said. "It might be better than a cottage. Think about it."

I could tell it appealed to Josh.

"This other thing," I said. "The sitting. I'm not sure I'm doing it right."

"Jesus Christ, Dad. You say that about everything. How can you do it wrong?"

"You can always call me," Jake said. "The real thing is just to do it. Don't make a big deal out of it."

"He already has," Josh said. "Believe me."

"Have confidence in the sitting. It takes you where you need to go."

7

THE PLAN WAS FOR ME and Jake to rendezvous in the evening, so I went for an afternoon swim. I'm actually a strong Y supporter, belong to them wherever I live, but the Cambridge Y was the exception. The locker rooms were ancient, shower rooms dank and moldy, fixtures crumbling, and the pool a twenty-yard wonder that took me back to my youth.

The great way is not difficult for those who have no preferences, as the saying goes. Unfortunately, I got 'em.

Worst of all, the toothless woman at the front desk, a sour look on her face, made me pay ten bucks to swim.

"I'm staying at this Y," I said.

"You're a guest resident. Not a membah."

"I have an away membership. I can use any facility."

"Not heah. We have our own policy. Pay up."

I asked to speak with the supervisor, but she was the supervisor. Probably pocketed the money.

Still, miraculously, the water was clear and cold. It was rather choppy, with six guys in three lanes, and took me eighty-eight lengths to make a mile. But I love swimming, the most meditative of all exercise, just you and the water, sounds drowned out, energy flowing. It always makes me feel better.

I had a scare when Jake didn't answer my knock; I used the

extra key but he wasn't there. He could have been anywhere, and I was ready to call out the National Guard when, unbelievably, I found him still at the bookstore, behind the counter talking to Morrie, the old guy who ran it. Morrie was thin and gray, had the worst posture on earth, but he loved Jake.

"You wouldn't believe this guy's stories about Japan," Morrie said.

"I might not believe them," I said, "but I've heard them. Dozens of times."

"You haven't heard his stuff," Jake said. "Peyote in Mexico. Some old blind guy who was a seer. A cowboy sitting full lotus."

"I *think* he was a real person," Morrie said.

Both men roared.

It was happy hour at the New Age rest home.

"What'd you do for lunch?" I said.

"Sent out for Chinese. Ate right here."

Jake had spent five and a half hours in that bookstore.

"Didn't you want a nap?" I said.

"Who can sleep, with this conversation?" Morrie said.

Who can keep from sleeping?

"Anyhow, old friend," Morrie said. The two men slowly stood. "You're our most cherished customer. Mazel tov." The two men embraced. There was something sad about it, though they were grinning like fools.

"My favorite bookstore on earth," Jake said.

"Maybe someday you'll buy something."

"Why buy, when you can read for free?"

That was the problem. It was more like a Christian Science Reading Room. Everybody just stood around. Some sat on the floor. Spiritual deadbeats.

We headed out.

"I'll turn you into a vegetarian yet," Morrie said. "Moo shu pork. *Mein Gott.*"

"Vegetables are sentient beings too. They scream when you slaughter them."

"Not like pigs."

These guys should have been on vaudeville.

"Someday I'll get you down to Mazatlán. The beautiful beaches. Magic mushrooms."

I sincerely hoped Morrie wasn't still doing that.

"Drugs cloud the mind."

"Clarify, clarify."

Jake slapped me on the back. "I'm ready for a beer."

Another roar from Morrie.

We stepped out onto Mass. Ave. The sun had gone down behind the buildings, just the slightest chill in the air.

Jake started to motor. He was making a beeline for someplace, not the Y.

"How was the afternoon?" I asked.

"Marvelous. Passed by in an instant. Like my life."

"Find anything to read?"

"Nothing you'd take home."

Jake had read everything at that point. He sometimes went back, like visiting old friends, but wasn't looking for anything.

"You're not tired? Don't want a rest before dinner?"

"I want a beer. I'll rest on a barstool."

This pre-dinner drink was an innovation. We never did that on Mount Desert.

I had to grab him, he was so intent on crossing Mass. Ave. His energy level seemed fine.

I wondered if he'd had any lapses at the bookstore. I doubted Morrie would have noticed.

We caused quite a commotion entering the bar. "Father Jake!" someone shouted, and there was a rumble of acclamation, guys turning with their best Japanese bows, hands pressed together. Jake, for his part, made the sign of the cross.

"Greetings, my children." They made way for us at the center, where we'd sat before. Jake took off his beret for Jess to kiss his head.

"I'm surprised she doesn't try to take it in her mouth," somebody said.

The middle finger flashed up.

"Don't listen to them, Padre. Guinness and a something. Can't remember."

"We know who she likes," somebody said.

"Just as well," I said. "I'm switching to Sam Adams."

"That I can remember."

I wondered if Jake had come here in the past. He'd never mentioned it.

Jess brought back our beers. She still had the black theme going big time, though her top was striped with gray. The streak in her hair and her nail polish seemed to have changed—was this possible?—to turquoise. My major impression about her wardrobe was that it was tight. She had the big boobs, a major butt. Her clothes emphasized those assets.

"How are you tonight, sweetheart?" Jake asked.

"Pretty good, Padre. A little foggy. Tuesday's rock and roll night. You guys should have stayed. There was a band."

"I'd have been lost. I don't go much past the Beatles."

"There's a special menu, smaller platters and cheap prices. It's a good night to eat."

"Wish I'd known."

"I was going to say, but you put down your beers and took off. I figured you'd hang more."

"We will tonight."

"Chill a little."

"We got in town yesterday. Had to get settled."

Jake had a way of looking past all the flaws in someone to see the real person. It was how he'd looked at Josh that first day, seeing the wild energy behind the awkwardness. He could talk to anyone, literally. I was surprised he'd picked out the bar maid.

There was another woman with her that night, and the waitresses hung around. Not much business in the restaurant. It was as if Jake created an island in the middle of the room where the two of them talked. People gravitated to him. I don't know how they knew.

"Why are you guys in town?" she asked.

"Leading a retreat, starting on Friday. A Zen retreat, seven days. Meditation all day."

"Sounds intense."

"It can be."

"My mother used to meditate. Did it every morning."

At that moment, as she said those words, Jake lost it. He looked bewildered, not there at all.

Jess hadn't noticed, talking over his head at the wall. "I always wanted to get into it. Never had the discipline. I'd like to now. But working at this place. Fuck. Pardon my French. This ain't exactly a monastery."

"Except that they brewed beer in monasteries, did you know that? In the Middle Ages?" It was the little guy from the other night, with the slippery glasses.

"I did not," Jess said.

"That's how they made their money. Monks also put a fair amount away."

"Maybe that's why they were fat," Jess said.

"And you," Jake said. "What do you do?"

I looked at him. Couldn't tell where his mind was. I'd put my hand on his back, to comfort him.

"How do you mean, Padre? I pump beer for these knuckleheads. Not you guys." She nodded to the little intellectual.

"But when you're not here." I thought he might be all right. He seemed to be back. He'd taken a long pull at the Guinness. "When you're not doing this. What do you do?"

"She gives blow jobs, Father."

It was a guy two stools down on the other side, big guy, big face, all florid.

You don't often see Jake angry. He doesn't have a mean bone in his body, nor an angry one. He knew it was just the beer talking, the guy joining in the banter. Not too subtle. But Jake also felt the meanness of the remark, putting Jess down. She had to be just a slutty barmaid.

Jess herself had blushed crimson.

"This is my conversation," Jake said, turning to the man. "We're having a conversation here."

I didn't see how Jake looked, but the guy got, if that was possible, even redder.

"Oh, right. I'm sorry. Sorry, Father."

He probably thought Jake was the parish priest. Just trying to be helpful.

"You were saying," Jake said.

"I don't really do much," Jess said. "This place keeps me busy. But I'm trying to go to art school. I want to go to art school."

"And do what?"

"Make jewelry. I like jewelry. You might have noticed."

I'd seen the nose ring, the multiple earrings. She also had three rings on each hand, a spangly necklace around her neck. God knows where else she may have been wearing metal.

"I did," Jake said.

"I'd like to make my own jewelry. Not just for me. Design jewelry. Have a line. I don't know. I don't know what I'm talking about."

"It's what you're interested in."

"What I'd like to do. I just think that's what I'd like. But I haven't done anything. Taken a class. I'm all over the place."

"Maybe next fall."

"That's what I was thinking."

"Classes start in the fall. You could take one. See if you like it."

"Yes." Jess smiled at the thought.

"I was in art school," Jake said.

"Really?"

"Before I did this. Then I went to Japan. Met some people. This took me over."

"I want to get into meditation too. Really like to. Come to that retreat. But I've got to work here. Shit."

"You can come to part of it."

"Part of the day?"

"Sure. Talk to Hank here. He can arrange it."

That was a unique aspect of Jake's retreats. In that way he was like his Japanese teacher. Many teachers said it was all or nothing—drop-ins were annoying—and of course in Japan it was often just monks. But Uchiyama let anyone come, with any time they had. He had a five-day *sesshin* once a month and sometimes people sat three deep; other times it was just one line. He said *zazen* was for everyone. Jake did too.

It made for some scheduling nightmares. And arranging for food? I didn't want to think about it.

"That's great," Jess said. "Thanks, Hank."

Think nothing of it.

"Right now I got to go. These guys need their beer."

"That's debatable," Jake said. "But we'll be back. You two can figure it out."

"Thanks, Padre. You're a doll."

Yet another lost cause for Jake. If I'd had to give my considered opinion, I'd have said that Jess wouldn't show up, wouldn't be able to sit still if she did. She wouldn't take that art class, wouldn't go to school, and would never start a line of jewelry. I wasn't at all sure the guy two stools down wasn't telling a simple truth. But Jake saw the person you deeply wanted to be. He treated you like that. Never failed to. Another trait I hoped to emulate.

He often got taken for a ride. That didn't stop him. And if he hadn't seen people that way—like that first day he saw me—I didn't know where I'd be.

Jake was down to his last swallow, finished it off.

"Korean okay tonight?"

"You lead the way." He knew the good places.

The crowd repeated their bows. Jake blessed them as if he were the Pope. The guy two stools down turned and apologized again; Jake shook his hand and patted his face. At this rate, the whole crowd would be showing up on Friday evening. The zendo would stink of beer.

The Korean place was up on Prospect Street, delicious noodle dishes, but so hot that my eyes watered. I had two beers, which made four for the day. Good grief. Jake made me have green tea ice cream for dessert. He had mango. We got back to the rooms and I sat *zazen* in a beery stupor.

8

IN THE MORNING when I sat my head was considerably clearer. I'd drunk several glasses of water before I went to bed, two more as I arose, and have to admit that, in the interest of convenience, I peed in the sink, a shameful habit my father taught me. When I finally left the room to take a shower—it was still early, a little after seven—I found my teacher sitting zazen in the hallway.

"Jake," I said. "What the hell."

This wasn't the first time he'd sat on a cement floor. That was the way he'd started in Japan.

"I went out to pee," he said, "then blanked out on my room number."

"Jesus Christ."

"Just couldn't remember. Got all turned around. Tried what I thought was the room and somebody was in there. Two guys, actually. One little bed."

And I thought this was a Christian organization.

"They weren't too happy," Jake said. "Thought it was a raid."

"Fuck 'em."

"*That* would have made them happy."

"When did this happen?"

"I don't know. Last night."

I wanted to say, "Why didn't you get me?" But of course he didn't know my room either.

"Don't you ever pee?" he asked.

I took him back and showed him my father's little trick, your cock over the edge of the sink, the hot water running. Jake would have to stand on a box.

"That's disgusting, Hank."

"Maybe. But half the guys in this place probably drink piss. And I wash the sink."

Jake shook his head.

"I want you to do this tomorrow night," I said. "No more *zazen* in the hall."

We went to the bathroom to shower and clean up. There was another guy in there—a skinny runt with a mustache, sloped shoulders—who kept turning to flash a hard-on at me. Jake didn't seem to notice, standing on the other side, but when we got to the room he spoke.

"I think that guy liked you."

"Seemed to. Anyway, Jake, this is the room. Stay till I come get you."

"If I need to pee I know what to do."

We got to the Golden D a little after eight. The same people seemed to be there. Same cigarette smoke. The scared skinny woman in the overcoat still didn't have anything in front of her. The man with the omelet was talking away.

I tried over easy that morning rather than scrambled, but the grease still won. I did switch to a muffin, and it was delicious, best thing there besides the coffee. Lily came to chat as we were finishing.

"You getting like Jake, Hank. You have muffin too."

"They're great."

"You getting like Jake. I can see." She pointed to her eyes.

I could only wish.

"You got girlfriend too, Hank? You getting girlfriend?"

"I think one is plenty between us."

"Maybe Jake find you one. His girlfriend got a friend."

There was an idea. Madeleine could fix me up.

"You need girlfriend, you be Buddhist. Need yin and yang."

"That's probably right."

"Chinese know. No girlfriend, you burn in hell."

Lily was getting close to home here.

Jake was standing from the stool. "There's always your buddy at the Y," he said.

"Plain donut good today, Jake. Very fresh."

He gave the thumbs up sign.

"You want plain too, Hank?"

"Can't do it Lily. I'm stuffed."

"You not Jake yet. He still the better man."

It was cooler that day on Mass. Ave., the sky cloudy. Not as many people out.

"You don't need to walk me," Jake said. "I can find it."

"I need to walk that breakfast off."

I wasn't about to let him go to Madeleine's alone after the night before. It really bothered me to find him sitting in the hallway in a T-shirt and undershorts. There is immense dignity in the *zazen* posture, especially when Jake does it, that rotund bald-headed body, sitting with his chin tucked in. He could sit by the hour, looked like a Chinese Buddha. There was a story about Sawaki sitting in an empty monastery as a young monk; the cleaning woman came in and kept bowing, not to him, but to that image. It was the simple posture of *zazen* that inspired her respect.

But Jake had also been just an old man sitting in the hallway in his underwear. It was cold out there.

"My butt's sore," he said after a while. We were walking slower than usual. "Sitting on that concrete."

"I wish I'd known you were there."

"In Japan, at *sesshins*, they had this weird custom. You were already getting zero sleep, three hours or so. Then when the day's sitting was over, you went out and sat in the garden, on a stone or something. It was like you were super-dedicated, couldn't get enough, except that everyone did it. You had to do it. It was required."

Jake had told me before. He'd told me most of his stories.

"Aching all over, dying to go to bed, and you had to go out and sit on a stone."

"Sounds crazy."

"Uchiyama did away with that. When the day was over, it was over."

You had just sat fifty-minute periods, of course. Fourteen of them.

We approached Madeleine's door.

"What are you going to do?" Jake asked.

"Go to a bookstore. Go watch chess. It's Cambridge. There's always something."

"You can play the chess master."

Jake and I played a lot in the winter, and he liked pitting his skill against the guy at Harvard Square. He never won.

"I can also throw my money down a sewer," I said.

"Madeleine's taking me to lunch. Some god-awful fancy place. I'll need a nap."

"I'll see you around five. You'll find your room all right?" We'd put a piece of tape on the door with the word Jake on it.

"If I can remember my name." He trudged up the steps. "Don't worry, Hank. People take care of me in this town."

Madeleine took care of him, that was for sure.

I just wondered what the guys at the Y would say when a Volvo with a driver dropped off one of their residents.

I walked back on Prospect, down the left, alongside those funky apartments, crowded streets with tiny houses, and when I first saw the young lady I drew a blank.

"Hank. How are you?"

"Great." I had no idea who she was.

"It's Jess. From the bar." She wore blue jeans and a sweatshirt, loose-fitting clothes for once, didn't have her gaudy make-up and jewelry. She looked completely different.

"Jess, holy shit, I'm sorry. You look different."

"I'm so embarrassed." She covered her face. "Don't even have makeup on. I feel naked."

"You look great." She was a nice-looking woman without all that crap on, taller than I, quite pretty.

"What are you up to? Where's Padre?"

"He's visiting a friend, a student of his, strong supporter. She's sponsoring this retreat. They're meeting and talking."

They wouldn't say two words about the retreat.

"And you?" she asked.

"I'm taking a walk."

"Want some company? I was just out for some breakfast. Didn't have any in the house."

"We can go somewhere."

"I'll walk. I'm not all that hungry. This is early for me."

It happened so quickly, so naturally, that I didn't notice how strange it was, an attractive woman less than half my age—ten years younger than my son—joining me for a walk. She hadn't put on makeup but wore perfume, one of those light fragrances younger women wear. She must have been four inches taller than I, even in flat shoes.

"The Padre's so cute," she said. "Like one of the seven dwarfs or something." I'd have to tell him. I'd tell him she said Dopey. "And so sweet, the way he talks to me. Does he talk to everybody?"

"No." That was an interesting subject, who Jake talked to. Like the way he focused on Josh rather than me that first time. "He picks people out. Seems to know who he wants."

"Why would he pick me?"

"Don't know." I'd wondered myself.

I'd taken us across Prospect and over to Harvard Street, my favorite. It was almost cold that morning, but I loved seeing the trees, smelling the autumn leaves.

"He's a monk, right?"

"Ordained priest, not a monk. It's a fine distinction. But he's not monklike."

"He is bald."

"He likes to be. Likes shaving his head. Hardly anything to shave anyway."

"Isn't it hard on you guys, living up there?"

"How do you mean?"

"I don't know. Maine. It's so remote. Just the two of you."

"Zen priests don't have to be celibate." I thought that's what she meant.

"They don't? So you're married?"

"We're not. We could be."

"That's what I mean. Living up there, no women around. Who lives in Maine, except some old dykes?"

That had been the whole point for me when I went. The remoteness.

"It's got to be lonely," she said.

"Anyplace can be lonely."

"The thing of it is, Hank." She took my arm. "What I mean to say. It's expensive living in Cambridge, holding one job. I try to get another, but there's nothing around. I'm always behind. Short on the rent. If I don't come up with a hundred bucks in the next day or so, my landlady'll be pissed. Throw my ass out."

"Damn."

"My place is back there near Prospect. We both have the morning free. We could have a good time."

It must seem stupid, but until that last sentence I had no idea what she was talking about. Of course some twenty-year-old woman would want to walk with me, ask about how lonely I was. Once I'd figured it out, it was all I could do not to stop in my tracks. I didn't want to seem indignant. I wasn't, actually.

The first thing I pictured was her giving a blow job to that big guy two stools down in the bar.

"I thought you were going out for breakfast," I said.

"I was. Honest to God. But then I saw you, and thought about the rent. It was the first thing I wondered about you guys, what you do for sex. I didn't think it was the two of you."

"No."

"Nothing wrong with that. But a woman gets a vibe, if a man's interested. The padre's sexy."

"I don't think there's a whole lot going on, to be honest."

"That doesn't mean he's not sexy. And you give off a major vibe."

I was hoping that wasn't true anymore.

"Would you offer an alcoholic a drink?" I asked.

"What do you mean? I give alcoholics drinks every day."

"But would you offer him one? If he didn't ask."

"You mean like tempt him? Maybe not. That'd be cruel."

"I know you didn't mean this, Jess. But you kind of just did. Offer an alcoholic a drink."

That stopped her. We kept walking, but she didn't speak for a moment.

"No, Hank," she said. "It's not the same. You don't get drunk. You don't get addicted. You don't wind up in the street. It doesn't even always cost money."

"It costs something."

"You older guys are uptight about sex. I don't know what happened to you. It's natural to fuck. Everybody does it. It's a good thing."

"Of course."

"That's what I mean about the vibe. I can tell you have that vibe. You need it."

Lily agreed.

"A woman can always tell. You need sex. I need to pay the rent. It's a good deal all around."

By that time we had stopped, were facing each other, standing at a cross street. She seemed utterly unembarrassed. At that moment, she seemed the older person.

"Is it really true about the rent?" I asked.

"Talk to my landlady. But not with me there, till I have my hundred bucks."

"Because this is a lot of money for me."

"You're getting a bargain, in this town."

"We've got to go to a bank machine."

"Of course."

"Then I want you to have breakfast. I'm buying."

"You're a romantic." She touched my face. "I could tell when we met."

I hadn't often been accused of that.

"You get the money," she said. "Help me with my rent. Then you can wine and dine me. We'll call it brunch. See what happens. But if you ask me." She winked. "I think you're going to get lucky."

Her favorite place to eat was at Inman Square. She didn't go there often because it was pricey, but it was a bright cheery place, a cut way above the Golden Donut, with large breakfast plates and a full bakery. Jess ordered a Western omelet and potatoes, a Bloody Mary—"I'm going to splurge"—and when I just wanted coffee seemed offended. "I can't eat alone."

"I had breakfast." A large greasy breakfast.

"He'll have coffeecake," she said to the waitress. "They have great coffeecake."

It also came in large hunks. The food on this trip would kill me.

For someone who said she wasn't hungry, Jess did all right. She ate slowly, and rather delicately, but ate everything. I was pleased that she sipped the Bloody Mary rather than knocking it back in two gulps and ordering another, which I was afraid she might. It seemed a big deal for her, going out for a meal.

"So tell me about art school," I said after the food arrived.

"Oh, art school. I don't know. That was something I said to Padre because he seemed to want me to. Have something other than pumping beer."

"So you made it up?"

"I've thought about it. I have this girlfriend who makes jewelry, a lot of the stuff I wear. She's talented when she's not stoned out of her mind, but makes zero money. Craft fairs, and one little store she sells to. It's not going anywhere. She never went to school."

"How far did you go?"

"Couple years of college. My mother made me. I had no idea what I wanted. Kind of resisted the whole thing. It's complicated. I'm still sorting it out. I was in this kind of prolonged fight with her. Then she got sick, and it all fell away. By that time I'd dropped out. That was good in a way, so I could take care of her. She died in June. Now everything's up in the air. I've been all kind of, fucked up. Which you would expect, I guess. I don't know. Jesus. How did we get started on this?"

She said these things between little bites of the omelet, small pieces of potato, spreading cream cheese on the bagel that came with every order.

"You sit there and nod," she said. "It all comes out. With a guy my age we'd be talking football by now. Sex."

"What about your father?"

"Mother was a lesbian. Lifelong. I grew up in a world of women. But I like guys. That was one of the things with her."

"She wanted you not to?"

"She didn't expect me to be a card-carrying dyke just because I came out of her. But she didn't like me getting wild. Drinking. Doing drugs. Being a normal kid. She had this whole egalitarian, save the whales, sit around and sing "Kumbaya" sort of mentality. Equal opportunity pussy eating. I don't know what she did with Stacey. But I don't think they strapped it on. Didn't want a thing to do with cocks, or anybody getting on top. But I love cocks. Which is where *you* come in." She leaned across the table. "Does it turn you on?"

"You turn me on. You're beautiful."

"Oh, Hank." She actually blushed, which she hadn't done during her diatribe. "I like you older guys. What about you? Got any kids?"

"One. He lives in Boston. Josh Wilder. He's a movie reviewer."

"No *way*. That guy for the *Globe?* I never miss his column. I even read the blog. He's your kid?"

I'd have to tell him he had a fan. Didn't know how I'd explain the circumstances.

"Does he have a girlfriend?" she asked.

"A number of them."

"Could I meet him?"

"I don't know, Jess. It's awkward."

"The father-son thing? I'd never mention it, swear to God. Jesus. Josh Wilder is your kid. I *love* his writing."

"You don't think he's slipping?"

"God no. Do you?"

"No. Writers get to thinking that."

"I bet I'm too young for him."

"Actually, you're not." You should be, but you're not. "I'll tell him he's got a fan at the Green Street Grill. He can drop by."

That was all Josh needed, to get hooked up with somebody like Jess.

"How about Padre? Does he have kids?"

"Not that he's mentioned."

"He's a sexy guy, though. I can tell. It's right there."

She wasn't the first woman to say something like that about Jake. I never understood. The sweetest man on earth, of course. Best listener, most understanding. All things women liked. But sexy? Exuding sexual energy? I couldn't see it.

By that time Jess had polished off everything. She'd had two cups of coffee, along with half of my coffeecake. She was a young big woman, but it was still surprising.

"Now I want another Bloody Mary," she said.

"You think that's wise?"

"This whole thing isn't wise. I usually just have toast and coffee. But it's a treat. The guys I know don't take me out. At least they don't pay."

"You should take yourself out. Don't wait for them."

The waitress, a tiny woman about my age, didn't approve of the second drink, but she hadn't been happy about the whole situation. I left a large tip. You could have eaten at the Golden Donut for a week on what I paid for that breakfast. We walked out to the square to find a teller machine, and I gave Jess the money.

"That's for your landlady," I said.

"You're sweet." She kissed my cheek.

"What time do you go to work?"

"Five. Four thirty if I want to eat. That won't be necessary today."

I'd been watching for any sign of a wobble while she walked, but she seemed fine. Might not have hit her yet.

"I'd still like to take that walk of ours," I said.

"You *are* romantic. Jesus. Not raring to go?"

"I'm enjoying myself. If you have the time."

"You like the younger woman thing. Being seen. You don't think they take me for your daughter?"

"You don't buy your daughter two Bloody Marys."

"I'll take your arm. I've got a buzz on. Probably look like I just fucked my brains out."

"You look great."

"That's what I mean. Lead on, Jeeves. I'm floating."

The streets down from Inman are nice too, as long as you stay away from Prospect, the sidewalks narrow and uneven, but that's from all the big old trees. We were strolling, not much in the way of exercise. Jess held my arm tight, but seemed to do fine.

When we'd turned onto Harvard and were heading toward the square, I said, "Tell me about your mother."

That made her stumble. She eased up on my arm.

"How do you mean?"

"What did she die of?"

"Breast cancer. Had it two years. The woman never smoked. Hardly drank. A glass of wine before dinner. She kept in shape. Kept her weight down. The last person you'd think would die."

I touched her hand on my arm.

"You wouldn't believe how god-awful it is to die of cancer," she said.

"So tell me about her. What did she do?"

Forty years ago, when I was sixteen and my father died, people had no idea how to handle grief, at least not the people I knew. My family didn't talk, went off alone with our grief, and those buried feelings poisoned my life for a long time.

I had one teacher, one wise man—I would never have picked him for wise, a science instructor and football coach—who came up to me in the gym, two days after the funeral, and said, "Tell me about your father," in front of a bunch of my friends. If more people had done that, over and over, if I'd just kept repeating the story, I might have absorbed it, been able to go on. Might have drained the poison. Instead of waiting fifteen years to do it with a therapist, then years of staring at a wall.

I might still have needed the therapy and wall-staring—maybe everyone does—but it would have eased things up, if more people had made me talk.

Jess's mother was a musician, a quiet woman named Paige

with a beautiful alto voice, but her real love was the piano, which she played at near concert-level ability. Maybe she was concert level, Jess didn't know, but she never gave concerts except for her friends at the house, and at the Unitarian church, and at a place in New Hampshire where they went for the summer. She also wrote her own compositions, which Jess thought beautiful but couldn't describe—"How can you describe music?"—couldn't classify as serious or popular. "I don't know. They were like nothing I've ever heard."

Her mother's partner was a lawyer who made most of the money, though Paige gave piano lessons and sometimes taught in schools. Stacey was the only other parent Jess had ever known.

"I never liked her. She wasn't warm and affectionate like Mother. She disapproved a lot when I got wild, never liked any of my boyfriends. Just didn't like men. Drove me crazy."

"She couldn't help you now?"

"What?"

"Go to art school. Take a class. Get things started."

"I don't see her. Don't want her money."

We had walked to the heart of the square, stopped to watch the chess master. He was a fair-skinned guy with a scruffy beard, wore a straw hat in the sun, had been playing at the square since Josh was little. He was agitated during a game, his leg vibrating like crazy, but had great concentration. He sat reading chess books when nobody played. And I'd seen him give free lessons to kids, endlessly patient with them, teaching strategy.

I liked anyone who lived out an obsession.

We walked around the square for a while, headed back toward Prospect.

"One thing about my mother would have interested you," Jess said.

"It all interests me."

"But the thing you'd really like was that she got up every morning to do yoga and meditate. Took her nearly two hours. Never missed. Still made it to the breakfast table before I got there."

"Where did she learn?"

"I don't know. It was a part of her life as long as I knew her. Which is why, though I may seem like an airhead who pumps beer for a living, a morning drunk who is about to give you the best blowjob of your life"—she actually didn't seem drunk; her cheeks were rosy, but her speech fine—"I really do want to come to that retreat. However much I can. I want to learn about it."

"Jake's a great teacher. You couldn't do better."

"I want to get my life in order. Something's wrong."

I knew the feeling.

We had made it back to Prospect by that time, turned down the little street Jess lived on. It was narrow and dead-ended into a playground, featured a bunch of tiny houses all alike, small stoops up to the door. Even then they were split up into duplexes, her place on the first floor.

"I live here with my girlfriend," she said, "but she works at a coffee shop. Doesn't get back till I'm about to go. The place is all ours."

The door opened onto a living room that was on the squalid side, a small ragged couch on one wall, two beanbag chairs in front of a TV, a sound system on the side wall, ashtrays full of butts, some beer cans on the floor, CDs and magazines scattered around. On the walls were posters of a couple of rock bands, both of whom looked simultaneously fierce and utterly ridiculous. Had these people ever heard of smiling?

"This is kind of grungy," Jess said. "But the bedroom's nice. I promise."

"I better not go back there," I said.

Jess turned. She had been walking ahead.

"I was glad to help with the rent," I said. "I wanted to. And I do like being seen with you. I liked our walk, and our talk. But as much as I'd like to, I can't go back there. It's not appropriate."

"Not *appropriate?*"

In your deepest place, Jake always said, you know what is right for any given moment.

"Just not right. Not something I can do."

Jess blushed all over. "Not appropriate is paying for two drinks at breakfast. Sitting there with a woman a third your age. Walking around with her on your arm. That's not appropriate."

"I liked all that."

"But now the fucking door is shut. You've walked in the door of my place, where I've come with God knows how many guys, and if anybody's watching, which I quite seriously doubt, if anybody's been watching this whole thing, they saw you come in here. That's the inappropriate part. But now that you're here, now that you've done all the risky stuff, you've even fucking given me money, you're not going to fuck me?"

"It's not that I don't want to."

"Do you have any idea how insulting this is?"

I just had to look at her to know.

"I have a tongue stud I put in to go down on guys," she said. "Wear it when I go on dates if I really like someone. Drives them fucking wild. You ever had that?"

"No."

"I'm about to put it in. You're not going to get past my mouth. Nobody does. We can do it right here." She grabbed my belt.

"You don't understand," I said.

"I understand when some guy says he's going to fuck me, pays my rent so he can do it, then when he gets here doesn't even try. What is it with you old guys? Are your dicks limp or what? You just want to be seen? Go home and jerk off with that?"

It was hard to talk to her, the woman was so furious.

"There's something in your life, right now, that you don't like, right?" I said.

"Lots of things."

"But there's something you want to change, something wrong, you just told me."

"Sure. I got a crummy job, fat guys with beer breath sitting there at the bar, looking at my ass with their tongues hanging out, while I give them beer to make them more drunk and more stupid. I live in this roach-infested fucking shithole where my bedroom is the one nice thing and you don't even want to see it. I live with my best friend but don't get to see her because we're working our asses off for no money whatsoever. And oh, one more thing, my mother died. I watched her go through hell for two years and watched her die. Those are the things I'd like to change. Can you change them?"

I wanted to take her hand, but it seemed too dangerous. If I gave her my hand she'd snap it in half.

"I mean the way you live," I said. "There's something you want to change."

"Maybe so. I haven't thought about it."

"Well for me, in my life, this was it. What I wanted to change."

"Making it with young chicks?"

"Young, old, everything in between."

"There's nothing wrong with that."

"It's not that it's wrong."

"It's a good thing to fuck. Everybody does it. It makes them happy."

"I had no control. It controlled me. I had to do it."

"Who cares?"

"It's a lousy feeling. Ruins everything."

"So you don't have to. I'm not saying you have to. You really don't have to. But you want to, don't you? It's fun."

"It doesn't matter how much fun it is. It's a bad feeling, when you have to. I can't go back to that."

It was the thing I'd spent years sitting and watching.

"So you never fuck?"

"I didn't say that."

"You'll never do it again? Jesus, I like you, Hank. I had a great time this morning."

"I did too."

"I might have done it without the rent money. Not that I would have spoken to you in the first place."

"So have breakfast with me again."

"You're hungry again?"

"Not now. Meet me again. Tomorrow."

"You want to date me?"

"I want to have breakfast with you. I'm paying."

"Then maybe the third or fourth time we do it, I bring along the tongue stud."

"Forget about sex. Leave that out of it. Have breakfast with me. Tomorrow. Ten o'clock."

"Why?"

"Because it was fun. Remember? Just a little while ago?"

"You do go home and jerk off with it."

"It's called being friends. It's a nice thing. People do it all the time."

"They do?" She put her arms around my shoulders, bumped her forehead against mine. "You are a sweet guy. It's hard to believe. Old enough to be my grandfather. I don't know what we're doing here, but I'll try. What the hell." She kissed my mouth lightly. "You sure you don't want me to just suck it a little?"

"Tomorrow, Jess. Ten o'clock. Breakfast."

9

JOSH AND I DID GO BACK to Mount Desert that second summer, stayed at the funky hotel. It was amazing how much he'd grown in the intervening year, not so much up—though he gained three or four inches—as out, his body finally catching up with his height. We rented bikes for the whole two weeks, hung around in town. I didn't see Josh a whole lot, actually. If it hadn't been for the movies, I might not have seen him at all.

He slept late, which gave me time to sit in the morning. I'd moved up from the fifteen minutes of the year before. We ate at the diner every morning, blueberry pancakes more often than not, sat at the counter behind the grill and tried to figure out their system, just two guys. They did the work of five.

After that I might not see Josh until dinner, or even the movie. He took his bike, but I didn't have the feeling he was making long forays into nature. We took one ride together toward the end of our stay, and he took me up that hill that had been so hard the year before, pulled way ahead of me. I had trouble keeping up.

At the end of the two weeks he told me he'd had a calzone for lunch every day, sampled every filling, and really wanted to get into the Dead. He'd been talking to the owners, and they'd played some stuff for him.

I spent much of the time alone. I took long bike rides, found a pool to swim in, spent hours reading. I also stopped in most days to talk to Jake (as did Josh, at different times). He was giving me books to read, and I attended the Thursday evening group, where we sat for a while and had a discussion. After trying on my own that whole year, it was a huge relief to talk to somebody who knew the practice, meet other people who did it.

At the end of our stay—the last two weeks in June, as it had been the year before—I stopped in one last time to see Jake.

"Josh is going off for six weeks with his mother," I said. "Soon after the fourth of July. Her family has a place in Canada, and they're all suddenly closer."

"I hope they have girls in Canada," Jake said.

"I don't know. The place is pretty remote."

"Josh is rocking."

Apparently he had reasons for visiting Jake alone.

"I'd like to come back here," I said.

"Oh?"

"The motel will give me a six-week rate. I like the island. And I want to study with you. If that's all right."

"Summers are tough. I'm busy in here. But we can get together in the evenings, now that you won't go to every movie. You can do a lot on your own. We don't have to spend hours. Checking in is helpful."

It had certainly been helpful for those two weeks.

"I want to pay for this."

"Either way. It's not important."

"This is what you really do. Not fixing bikes."

"I fix bikes so the teaching won't get mixed up with money. This place is my job. The rest is just life."

I hadn't had any idea I'd want to do such a thing when I arrived that summer. It was a sudden impulse, but I couldn't get it out of my mind. It was as if I'd been starving for something all my life and had finally found it. I couldn't give it a name. But I knew it was feeding me.

I thought we might meet formally—I'd heard of Zen teachers and students sitting head to head—but Jake preferred long strolls, around town or up in the park. He also loved simple social occasions, going out for a meal or for coffee. He thought them as sacred as anything in life.

He looked largely the same in those days, already bald and shaving his head, big chested and slightly rotund, slightly heavier if anything. But he was a vigorous man, exuded energy, a physical person who loved the outdoors. Sitting for him was first and foremost a physical act. Buddhism was something you *did*, with your body.

"The thing I've been wondering," I said on the first evening after I'd come back, "is whether it's appropriate to work on something in sitting, the way you might in therapy. Pick something out."

"I'm not sure 'work' is the word," Jake said. "You don't want to be too active, or too intentional. If it's important, it comes up."

"It comes up."

"What is it?"

"Women."

Jake couldn't suppress a smile. "The fruit falls close to the tree."

"It doesn't seem the same with Josh. I was nothing like that. Wish I could have been."

"Don't glorify it too much. He has his problems."

Everybody came to Jake for help.

"This is what broke up my marriage," I said. "If I had to pick one thing."

"Other women."

"Yes."

"But you're free now. How long's it been?"

"A year and a half."

"Have you tried being really free? Just letting it rip?"

"I have."

"And?"

"I have three women, I want four. Four, I want five. It gets more and more tangled. I'm ready to become a monk."

"Because monks are happy?"

"Aren't they?"

"Some are and some aren't. About like the rest of us."

We just walked for a while, down a street of shops that gave way finally to a street of houses, small cottages. Jake walked with his hands behind his back, his little tummy sticking out.

"What do *you* do about this?" I asked.

"Women?"

"Yes. Were you ever married?"

"When I was younger. Before I went to Japan, and started practice. Then I knew some women in Japan. I've been with a few since I've been back. The problem has never been sex for me. I can take that or leave it."

That was a totally incomprehensible statement to me.

"The problem for me is finding someone who understands what I do. Women aren't beating down the doors to get with a guy who works in a bike shop."

"That's not what you do."

"But practicing Zen. Having a handful of students. It's not much of a career."

Maybe not. But it was extraordinarily valuable.

"The whole way I live. Turning in early. Getting up in what seems like the middle of the night. This devotion to practice. Women might go along with it for a while. Even want to do it with me. But they don't finally understand that it's the first thing in my life. They get in competition with it. Want me to compromise."

"Your students understand."

"That's tricky. Some of them are interested. But they think I'm some saint. Turns out I fart and scratch my balls like all the other guys."

Even I idealized him. It was hard not to.

"The thing about sex," he said. "This thing you're bringing up. Becoming a monk, whatever, wouldn't end the problem."

"I wasn't entirely serious."

"Priests in Japan aren't celibate. They're allowed to marry. But they refrain while they're training. Still, the young guys I knew at my first temple were jumping each other all the time. Going to whores if they could scrape up the money. Jerking off like crazy. It was like boys' boarding school."

"What about Uchiyama?"

I didn't know Jake's whole history at that point, but he had spoken sometimes of the man he considered his true teacher.

"He just wanted people to sit. Didn't look at their private lives. He was married himself. To his third wife."

I had to hear more about this guy.

"I don't know if there is such a thing as a true celibate," Jake said. "Who doesn't even masturbate, just recycles the energy. It seems possible theoretically. I'm not sure I get the point. I do know we tend to idealize people, especially people we think of as holy, especially from the ancient past. I don't know what the Buddha did about sex. What Jesus did. But if they were human, they dealt with it."

It didn't seem a highly charged subject for him.

"I wouldn't make rules about it, like you'll give it up for such and such a time. That sets up a conflict. Just sit a lot. Try to be mindful in daily life, the same thing I'd tell anyone. See what you get hooked by, if that's what hooks you, and try to stay awake. You'll screw up sometimes. You've got to take it easy on yourself. Try to learn from it."

It seemed simple advice, the next thing to nothing.

"Mostly I'd sit a lot. Just be aware and look at it."

The ironic thing about that conversation was that I'd started to get involved with Madeleine and, unbeknownst to me, she told Jake everything. I was talking about being celibate while, with another part of my mind, I was putting it off. It was the Make Me Chaste But Not Yet situation. The secret hope was that *this* woman would be the one who understood, *this* would be the one it all worked out with. There was no problem after all! I just hadn't found the right person!

I didn't have her to the motel, of course; we met strictly at her place. I didn't even take her to the diner for pancakes. But it was the classic situation: we fell into bed almost immediately, made love as if we adored each other. Soon she saw my neediness and fear. I saw her limitless yearning for affirmation. Skip the engagement and the wedding: we can jump right to the divorce. It didn't even last six weeks.

I did sit a lot in the morning, though Jake cautioned me not to turn it into an athletic event. In the afternoons I exercised and spent time with Madeleine. The evenings I gave to her. Time passed quickly.

Sex started to come up big time when I began doing retreats, which didn't happen until the following year. Jake in the summer just had classes and the sitting group, where he taught a lot of newcomers. But during the rest of the year he scheduled retreats at times when people were likely to be free, Christmas and spring break, and his loyal students made the trek up to what was then Madeleine's house, would eventually be his.

She herself didn't do retreats. She came to the island, sat a period or two every day and came to the talks, but never tried the whole thing. She was sure she couldn't, had a dreadful fear of it. Even now, twenty years later, she hadn't sat a whole retreat.

I found my morning mind clean and clear, often felt full

of energy. Right before lunch Jake gave a talk, which often inspired me. After lunch was a work period. But in the late afternoon, when the energy wasn't strong anymore and the day looked long—it was three o'clock, say, and we wouldn't do anything but sit and walk until bedtime at ten—in that time of low energy and discouragement, when the room seemed small and close, fantasies arose. I'd been seeing them all my life.

"Just watch," Jake said, when I told him. "Don't think about them, analyze them, try to figure them out. Just see them."

They were the images I'd always comforted myself with, when I was afraid, frustrated, unhappy. Mostly afraid. They'd been extremely dependable, muffled the fear entirely.

Now when another kind of fear was coming up—or maybe it was the same, maybe all fear is just of that endless stretch of time, endless space, nothing at all to fill it, the reality of existence that we face on long Sunday afternoons when there is nothing to do—they arose again.

"I'd like to meet the fear," I said to Jake. "These things are in the way."

"They are the fear," he said. "The fear and the distraction are the same thing."

It was like being locked in a tiny porn theater where the same loop of film ran again and again. You couldn't get away no matter what you did. It showed on the screen, on the walls, in the balcony.

This is your life, Henry Wilder.

I'm not talking one retreat. I'm talking multiple retreats, over a number of years, even some I did with other teachers.

"Afternoons are more yang," one teacher said (or maybe it was yin; I don't remember). "It's natural for sex to come up, for a certain kind of person."

I was that person in spades.

"I have a friend who lives in Africa," another said. "There you might have two or three wives. Visit different ones on different days. That's how they deal with the problem."

It had gotten to the point where Jake, when I brought it up, would just say, with a smile, "That's your specialty." One time, in the late nineties, when a certain event dominated the headlines, he said, "Maybe you should run for president." Then, in an afterthought, "If he had just listened to Joycelyn Elders, we might have avoided this whole thing."

Finally, after years of trying to deal with those afternoons, hearing Jake brush them aside, we were sitting in *dokusan*—the interview that a student has with his teacher, sitting cross-legged, knee to knee—when I said, "I'm tired of these fantasies. I want them to end."

For once that brought out the fierceness in the man, and his certainty.

"No." He leaned forward. "This is your conditioning. This is your karma. You have to see this. The nature of desire."

The nature of desire (in case you want to skip all the sitting) is that it is endless. You want sex and want sex and want sex and want sex. After that you want sex for a while. If you actually have sex, then you want a cigarette, or to smoke a joint, or take a nap, whatever you like. Then you want a bowl of ice cream. Some cookies might be nice. Why don't we brew some coffee? As you're sipping the coffee, coming back to life, you think, maybe it would be nice to have sex again.

If you feel superior to this, if you're a woman and this sounds childish perhaps or *just like a man*, substitute shopping. Substitute food. Shoes. Alcohol. Rapt adoration. Sooner or later you'll find your thing. Or just sit for days at a time. It'll show up.

I spent my summers in Bar Harbor—Josh coming up when he could—for the next four years. When Josh went to college—in Boston, as it turned out—I moved to the island and taught at a high school, began to help out at the bike shop in the summers. In recent years I'd been able to quit the teaching job, become a full-time student and assistant to Jake. Basically he supported me, with *dana* from his students and a lot of help from Madeleine. Also that huge summer rent on the house. For much longer than that I'd ordered my life around continuing this practice. I didn't have another life. This was my life.

10

I STILL HAD MUCH of the day left when I left Jess's house in the middle of the morning. Jake would be coming back after a late lunch to take a nap. I went to the bookstore for a while. It was amazing what you found in there, obscure texts from thirty years ago, when Zen was just getting started in this country. There were actually chairs where you could sit and read. I don't think Morrie cared about selling books. He just wanted to help seekers on the path, as he would put it. He loved it when some fresh-faced kid came in with a question. And he lived to debate old hands like Jake.

He seemed not to recognize me, which was just as well. I bought a couple of paperbacks just to keep the place going.

I had a quesadilla and some limeade, walked down to the square to watch more chess. It was a completely different game at that speed; you had to react instinctively, read your opponent in a move or two. There were guys in Cambridge who lived to beat the chess master. He was the fastest gun in the west.

I wondered what kind of safety net Jess had. She lived in that shabby apartment, which nevertheless probably had a steep rent. She no doubt made a fair amount in tips as a bar girl, unless all the regulars took her for granted. She wasn't getting rich, that was for sure, and she couldn't do that forever. She didn't have a college degree or much motivation to get one.

Maybe she was a part-time hooker who, taking care of all the regulars at the Green Street Grill, made a ton of money. Maybe she was supporting a drug habit, didn't need the money for rent at all. Maybe she had a boyfriend who adored her and would take her off someplace to raise kids and she was just waiting until he got his start.

One thing I did know was that she wasn't terribly far—losing her job, or having her roommate move out, or having an accident—from the homeless people you saw hanging around the square. There wasn't a huge distance between the waitresses at the Green Street Grill and the lost souls who hung around the Golden Donut. Just twenty years or so—which pass in the blink of an eye—and a few bad breaks.

I also knew that two months after my father died I was a zombie, didn't know what I was doing. Ten months later I wasn't much better. It was a terrific shock, with a long recovery time.

I walked to the Y after a while and took a swim. Didn't get into a big thing with the woman at the desk, just paid my ten bucks and went down.

Jake was still asleep when I knocked on his door. He was glad I came when I did, didn't want to nap too long.

"Madeleine's serious about these plans for the center," he said. "Ready to knock out a wall for a bigger office. Took me to look at furniture. I had no idea she was this far along. You've got to decide if you're up for this."

He was moving around the room getting his clothes on. That was a hell of a way to greet me.

"What about you?" I asked. "You'll be moving from a place you've lived thirty years."

"Be realistic. We're not talking about me. We're talking about a commitment for the rest of your life."

Let's not knock down the wall just yet.

Jake pulled on a jacket. "Ready for a beer?"

We walked down the stairs and out onto Mass. Ave. The evening was dark, had turned cool.

Jake seemed fine when we stepped out the door, but by the time we got to the corner his eyes went vacant. He seemed not to know where he was, where we were headed. I took his arm at the light and walked us to the other side. He stopped at the familiar storefront. "Fishcakes and beans are good here."

Dinner at the Golden Donut? I don't think so.

"What about that beer?" I said. "Don't you want a beer?"

"Oh, right."

"We're going to Green Street."

He didn't seem to know where that was.

I pulled him to the right, walked us back there. "The boys are waiting for you," I said.

The crowd went wild when Jake walked in, and that seemed to bring him back; I don't know whether he reacted spontaneously or was remembering, but people did their best little bows and he blessed them all around. "Clear the stools, clear the stools," everybody said; they put us in the same spot we'd occupied the last two nights, right in the center. It was a big crowd, guys standing two or three deep, lots of talk, music playing.

Jess had our beers by the time we sat down. Jake lowered his head for the ritual kiss. She wore a big smile. The streak in her hair was scarlet. I could have sworn she'd changed it since that morning.

"Padre," she said. "Would you believe what happened? Some guy took me to breakfast and bought me *two* Bloody Marys. Two drinks before ten o'clock."

"I wonder what he had in mind."

"Only one thing. I fended him off."

"That was a first," somebody said.

"It is *weird* having a hangover in the middle of the afternoon," she said. "I shouldn't have taken a nap."

"You shouldn't have taken the drinks. Listen, sweetheart. I talked to a friend. An old friend, very generous person, has helped me with a lot of things. She's willing to stake you to that art class. Help you find your way to school if you want."

Jake was going out of his way for this young lady.

"Jesus, Padre." For the first time since I'd known her, Jess looked flustered. "That's sweet. So unexpected. I don't know if I can do it."

"How so?"

"It's just," she shrugged, "I don't know if I can do it."

"One way to find out."

"I know, Padre. But Jesus. Somebody's paying. I try and I screw up."

"This woman has a lot of money. Not a big deal to her."

Jess wiped the bar with her rag. It didn't need wiping.

"I don't know, Padre. If you say so."

"You can at least meet the woman. She's coming to the retreat. You're still doing that?"

"I want to. Yes." She didn't seem as sure.

"You decide what hours and tell Hank tomorrow night. He'll arrange everything."

"All right, Padre. Listen, there's a lot of thirsty people here."

"Of course. You've got a job." He raised his glass.

"I appreciate this. You can't know."

She blew him a kiss and walked away. He swallowed, I would swear, half a Guinness in one hit. He had a hell of a capacity for a little guy. I'd never seen him even close to drunk.

I was surprised he'd brought Madeleine in on that. It would be pocket change to her, but I didn't think she'd want to put every barmaid in Cambridge through college. Still, he was like that. We'd be having a conversation in a café somewhere and some guy would overhear and ask about Buddhism. Jake would stand there for forty-five minutes, running through the whole thing. A homeless guy would ask for money and Jake would give him fifty cents and listen to his whole life story (no doubt made up), tell him about shelters, places he could get food. All the guy probably wanted was the nearest liquor store.

"We should talk about this center," I said, having put down half my beer. Had to keep up.

"Let's save it for dinner. It's so noisy in here."

It was as if the beer were strictly incidental. He'd come to deliver the news.

I felt weird enough about the whole episode with Jess that I wasn't telling him. At no moment had I had any intention of having sex with her. As soon as she'd mentioned it, my only feeling was that I didn't want to make her feel bad, had to decide if she really needed money for rent (a fifty-fifty chance). I sure as hell didn't want to see her bedroom. I actually think sex is every bit as wonderful as she seemed to, didn't think it was wrong to pay for it. I'd paid for it in the past. If she got me to the bedroom I was in trouble. But I wasn't at a point in my life where I wanted to go with a twenty-year-old girl who picked me up on the street.

Jake and I ate at a Chinese restaurant at Inman Square, right on the corner of Prospect. It was a tiny place, hardly big enough for a restaurant. We sat at a table at the window, looked on the street. Only two couples were there. A big relief from the noisy bar we'd staggered out of.

"I think Madeleine pictures you heading the center," I said. "No matter how many times you tell her."

"Probably right."

"She isn't doing it for me."

We were sharing moo shu pork and a platter of Chinese

broccoli. Jake waited while the server made a little taco for each of us. He sipped his tea.

"She's always wanted me down here," he said. "But I love the beauty of the island. The quiet life. I don't think it matters how many students you teach. It's how you do it, what influence they have. You can carry my teaching on."

He'd never said that to me before, and I'd honestly never thought about it, until that trip to Cambridge.

"You're my dharma heir," he said. He was trying to hammer it home.

"I don't know, Jake." Big shoes to fill.

He seemed not to hear, making another taco. He threw on a little broccoli for good measure.

I'd never met anyone else who enjoyed food the way Jake did. He could do without: in Japan he'd lived for years on rice and pickled vegetables, and up on the island we had a simple diet, didn't take much trouble. But even at *oryoki*, the ritualistic meal we ate at retreats, when the pot came around he held out his bowl with a huge smile, as if at a gourmet feast. Bean soup for the millionth time. He loved the greasy eggs at the Golden Donut the same way he loved this moo shu pork, which was first-rate. He didn't literally have just one bowl, like the monks in the old days, but was grateful for anything that plopped into it.

"I read something once that fascinated me," he said. "I think it was that wild Tibetan who fucked all his students. He thought the Buddha didn't set out to teach. Have you heard this?"

"No."

"The usual view is that he got enlightened and faced this decision, whether to stay in the forest or go off and teach. He decided to teach, like a professor deciding on a career.

"But this guy thought he didn't do that. He just joined the world, the situations arose, and he taught out of them. He didn't have a system, didn't have an intention. He just saw people suffering, and tried to help them."

Jake always taught to a situation, one way or another.

"That's the way to teach," Jake said. "Don't plan. Let it come up."

Like it or not, that was what I'd be doing in those lectures.

"What if nothing comes?"

"Say nothing."

That would go over big.

"I also think, I've always thought, that giving talks is the least of it. Uchiyama didn't give talks."

There was a solution.

Jake hadn't known what to do with himself when he came back from Japan. It was the early eighties, and several centers had established themselves. He wandered around trying to fit in. He might have stayed in San Francisco if Shunryu Suzuki had still been there, but he'd died years before. Rochester was possible, but that was another teacher, another system.

He didn't think the teachers he encountered were wrong. But he'd had a particular experience, couldn't find anything that seemed similar. He wondered sometimes if something was wrong with him, but had to trust his deep feeling. The last place he tried was in Maine. The end of the line.

When that didn't work out he went up to Mount Desert and got a job, practiced on his own and taught classes. The nature of the practice is that 80 percent of the people who try it—already a bold group—don't stick with it. That made for paltry numbers at first. Even when I went, there were just five or six loyalists, Madeleine among them.

"I'm not worried about you," Jake said. "Whatever happens."

Wished I could say the same.

"It's Madeleine I worry about," he said.

"Madeleine?"

We were obviously talking about different things. I was thinking money.

"If it weren't for Madeleine, we wouldn't be sitting here. I'm not at all sure I'd be teaching."

Almost as soon as Jake and Madeleine met, she let him occupy the garage apartment, rent free. When she left in the winter she made him caretaker, paid him a salary. Eventually she'd bought another house and let him keep the first one and take the income from it in the summer. It was a big break for him, a most generous act.

He seemed genuinely troubled by this subject. He seemed to fade away for a while. I wondered sometimes if certain topics brought his problem on. He had stopped eating—always a bad sign—sat quietly, staring at the table. Then the light came back to his eyes.

"We don't understand, because sitting was easy for us," he said.

"Speak for yourself."

"I don't mean that stuff at first. Sore back and sore knees. But I knew when we met that you would stick with this. Your posture was lousy, body all tight. Posture still isn't great."

Another reason not to teach. They were adding up.

"You were a troubled human being. I knew there was something here for you."

He'd known more than I had.

"Madeleine had beautiful posture the first time she sat." He smiled. "Maybe because she'd done yoga, or been a dancer. It was exquisite."

I could use her as a model. Listen to me, look at her.

"She just can't do it. All these years later."

That was the thing I couldn't fathom.

"I always had the feeling the basic teaching was true," Jake said. "Buddha nature, true self. There was a genuine person in there who would just emerge, if you could get past all the crap. That made sense the first time I heard it."

For me too.

"Madeleine's afraid of what's in there. Doesn't see the true self. What's standing in the way is so vast, so troubling."

She had her demons, that was for sure. You just had to go to bed with her—hate to mention it—to see them. Most women lie around forever afterward. She bolted like she was scared to death. Some phony excuse. She'd let you stay but was a terrible sleeper, wandering the house half the night. It was like sleeping alone.

"The funny thing is," I said, "that her true self is right there. She's the sweetest person you'll ever meet."

"I know. And a model of devotion. She'd give me her last dollar, if it came to that."

That'd be the day.

"The problem is," he said, "she's devoted to *me*. Has this idea I keep her alive. What if I'm not here?"

She wouldn't transfer that to me.

"This practice isn't about sitting," he said. "It's about compassion, which can't be taught. I've never helped Madeleine sit. She's been the biggest puzzle of the past thirty years. But compassion. Where you naturally feel for the person, reach out to help. She teaches that to me."

11

AT THE GOLDEN D the next morning I had just a muffin, the perfect solution. The coffee was superb, the muffin fresh and delicious, and I wasn't overwhelmed.

Lily sidled over. "Hank not feeling well. Not eating today."

"I don't know what's wrong with him," Jake said.

"I'm fine, really. I like these muffins. Don't want to distract myself."

"Maybe have donut today. Very fresh. Still warm."

"This is all I want."

She shook her head and walked away. I'd never be the man Jake was.

The omelet man was holding forth. He did seem to be a fine orator, with considerable dignity, though I couldn't catch the actual words. It was amazing the way people around him sat as if nothing were happening. The scared woman in the overcoat had a glass of water today. She was the one person in the room I might have advised to *take up* smoking. I really wished she would do something.

At what seemed the ultimate moment in his discourse, the omelet man took a bite of his omelet, stared at it in horror, and tossed it into the wastebasket directly in front of him, on the other side of the counter. Poured his coffee in for good measure.

"Does that woman want some food, Lily?" Jake asked as we left.

"She just want sit. Sit all the time."

"She wouldn't eat if I bought it for her?"

"We try. Not want food. Just sit."

There weren't too many places that would have let her.

"Chocolate donut good today, Jake."

Jake beamed. Chocolate was his favorite.

"You take care of Hank. He stop eating too. Pretty soon just like her. Sad face, glass water."

We stepped out to the avenue. The cold from the night before had lingered, but the day was brilliant and bright, just a few white clouds in the sky. We were wearing our jackets. Autumn was settling in.

"What a donut," Jake said. "My God."

It was a chocolate cake donut with chocolate icing.

"You should go back and get one. I'm not kidding."

"I don't eat dessert with breakfast."

"Why not?" He was perfectly serious. "We're on vacation."

Jake considered any trip a vacation. Actually, his whole life was a vacation.

I put an arm around him and gave him a squeeze. The man was irrepressible.

We headed toward Hampshire. He had apparently slept better, wasn't dragging like the day before.

"You can come in," Jake said as we got near Madeleine's. "She'd like to see you."

"We've been over that," I said. Madeleine was the soul of politeness, but always was disappointed if she wasn't alone with Jake. The time they had alone was different, and helped her somehow. She guarded it jealously.

"We've got to talk logistics about the center," Jake said. "Sometime."

"There's plenty of time for that."

"I'm not going to be the one to pick out office furniture," he said. "I can tell you that."

There was something I never thought I'd be doing.

Madeleine waited for us at the front door. "I do think we should talk soon," she said when she heard I was leaving. "How about tomorrow morning? I can talk to Darcy about the food." Madeleine had volunteered her cook to handle the retreat.

"Tomorrow it is," Jake said. "She can make some more of those cookies."

Darcy was a big Irish woman, threw food at you whenever she got a chance.

I had time for a walk before I met Jess. I headed toward Harvard, figured I'd circle around and come back. I loved that kind of crisp fall morning. Autumn was my favorite season in New England.

I was like Jake, hadn't realized things were so far along in Madeleine's plans. I knew we were finally, after all these years, coming to do a retreat in Cambridge, as she'd always wanted. I also knew that Madeleine wanted to lure Jake down there for good, have a place for him to teach full time. I was vaguely aware she'd had her house in mind for that purpose. But I thought she'd have done something much more makeshift at that point, move furniture out of one room temporarily. I'd never thought she was fully engaged in transforming the place, had already—as Jake mentioned the day before—put down a deposit on a condo for herself. It was as if she were trying to steamroll things through: if she got the place ready, he had to come. She was a shrewd person and a good businesswoman. If she was behind it, it would be first rate.

I wasn't afraid, as Jake seemed to be, of the administrative side. I wasn't even worried about living in the building where the center was. Jake and I were both part hermits. The setup at Mount Desert was just about right for us. But we'd adjust.

The thing that scared the bejesus out of me was the whole thing of being a teacher.

He'd given me everything he had. We'd gone over the classic texts of Soto Zen. He'd put me through lay ordination, then a small priest ordination a few years before. But I'd done all that in the context of being his sidekick. I hadn't seen it another way.

The true thing that a teacher passes on, the truest thing, Jake had given me just by my being around him, the love and compassion that permeated his person. He was not a perfect human being. You couldn't live with someone for years and not see his imperfections. In that way Madeleine was lucky he hadn't fallen for her, and Jake was right to avoid it (I was utterly convinced that anyone who got into bed with her became that person she had to flee. He would have lost his whole aura in the space of a few minutes).

The thing I'm talking about he had the first day I met him, when he watched Josh pitch a fit as if he were singing an aria. That was the day that made me want to study with him, even before I knew what he taught; I wanted to discover wisdom that manifested as compassion. There was no splitting them apart. They were one thing.

I still thought after all those years, even after being exasperated at him on numerous occasions, that he was the sanest, sweetest person I'd ever met, made others saner and sweeter by being around them.

A person would have to be blind not to see he was getting older, or that something was happening to what the world would call his mind. "Firewood becomes ash," Dogen Zenji said, "and it does not become firewood again." But the profound presence that made Jake different from most people was there just as much after his episodes began as it was there before. I believed it would be there if he were totally blotto. And inasmuch as I'd thought about the future, all I'd really decided was to stay with him until the end. Past that I hadn't figured.

Jess, when I met her that morning, had yet another look, a short blue skirt and purple pullover sweater. She did still have the nose ring and several dozen earrings, but wasn't as garish with the makeup, didn't look like a budding vampire. She was sitting at a booth and rose to kiss my cheek when I arrived. It was as if she'd gone to charm school.

She didn't even offer to blow me for a hundred bucks.

"No booze today," she said. "I'm a changed woman."

Our little waitress—we had her again—smiled broadly.

"Yesterday morning was a dream," Jess said. "The afternoon a nightmare."

"And I'm eating today," I said. "I took it easy with Jake." I wanted an egg that didn't taste like day-old grease.

After we ordered, Jess said, "This thing about art school. Taking a class. It's gotten out of hand."

"I thought you looked a little shocked."

"I was just talking. To say something."

"It came from somewhere."

"It's one of those things girls say when they're sitting around. I ought to go to art school and start a line of jewelry. Lose thirty pounds and become a model. Take up the bass and start a rock band. It's not like you're going to do it."

"What did you study before, when you were in school?"

"Nothing. That was the problem."

"What were you supposed to study?"

"I don't know. Liberal farts. What everybody does. What's the point?"

Josh had hung around artsy types without career ambition. It was fine if their parents were around, or they had a dependable boyfriend, a little money in the bank. What was scary—if it was true—was the thought of her scraping by for the rent every month. Even though—as that fat guy on the barstool suggested—she apparently had a viable skill that was much in demand.

"My mother was never like that," Jess said. "Not for one minute of her life, I'm convinced. Things might not have worked out the way she wanted. But she always wanted to do music, from the time she was little. Practiced the same way, hours every day. She didn't push me into music, which was good. But she wanted me to find something like that. That kind of passion."

"It's intimidating."

"You said it. Not just the passion, the intensity, day after day. I was proud of her. But I didn't have that. I didn't see how anybody could. How could you be that way?"

It was more or less the way Jake was about all of life.

Our food arrived, another omelet for Jess, eggs over easy for me, potatoes that seemed just to have been cooked rather than sitting around on a grill drying out, fresh fruit, a warm bagel and cream cheese. The orange juice was fresh squeezed.

I wondered if I could drag Jake up here.

We ate for a while, enjoying the food.

"My mother used to play things for me when I was a little girl," Jess said. "Sometimes her own, sometimes other people's. I didn't know the difference, though I used to play a game, trying to guess what was hers. It was like playing, two kids playing. The music just rolled off the piano. Those were some of the sweetest moments of my life."

"Did she play for her partner?"

"Didn't have a partner then. It was just the two of us."

I didn't want to say much, it all sounded so delicate.

"The funny thing was, after Mother got sick, all her anxiety about performing went away. She gave a concert before she died, big crowd at the Unitarian church, played only her own compositions. It was fantastic, she didn't seem nervous at all. Pumped up and radiant, but not nervous. I never heard anything like it, even when I was a girl. It was like seeing the person she could have been."

She put her head down and cried. She didn't sob, but tears streamed from her eyes, her chest heaving. "Fuck," she said.

We were sitting in a booth in the far corner. Jess had her back to the place, and hardly anyone was there. Our little waitress had been barreling in our direction with a coffeepot, but I waved her off. I reached over and took Jess's hand.

"It's all right, Jess. There's nobody here."

"I know. It's just too . . . I haven't talked about this."

"It's good to talk."

"I know, but Christ. Bawling into my eggs at a restaurant."

"You're not the first, I'm sure." The place catered to neurotic intellectuals. People probably cried there all the time.

She took out a handkerchief and wiped her eyes, blew her nose. She blew again.

"Feels good, actually." She laughed.

"I wish I'd known your mother," I said.

"She didn't know a lot of guys. Didn't know a lot of people period. Her thing was women. Didn't hang out with men. She knew what you're after, with those fat dicks of yours."

We both laughed. The crying seemed to be over.

I nodded at the waitress, who'd been hovering with the coffeepot. She came and poured.

"You all right, honey?" she asked. "Maybe you should of had one of them drinks."

"I'm fine," Jess said. "We're fine."

She sipped her coffee.

"I'm convinced the whole thing, everything she did, came out of that stuff in the morning. Yoga and meditation. She had a special room for that, this small bright room in one corner of the house, where she did those things. The one came out of the other."

That was true and it wasn't. Meditating was no guarantee

you'd produce anything. It didn't make you an artist. It was its own thing.

At the same time, Jess was right. The art did come out of the meditating.

"So I want to do it," she said. "But I'm also scared."

"Everybody's scared," I said.

She gave a huge shudder, shook all over.

"Why are *you* scared?" I asked.

"Because it means I'm serious," she said.

"Really?"

"About life." She shook her head. "You know what I mean? I'm going to buckle down and do it. Really live my life. Quit farting around."

"Yes."

"Mother was so serious. She was fun too. But she had this serious side. She was just going to do it. That's why it wasn't so sad when she died. I knew she had lived her life."

"That's wonderful."

"But what if, like, Lauren, my roommate, my best friend, comes home and finds me *meditating*?"

"What if she does?"

"It's like I was praying, or something. Beating off."

"Women call it beating off?"

"This woman does."

You learn something new every day.

"It's so private," she said. "So embarrassing."

"So do it in your room. Do it when she's not there. You can tell her you do it, right?"

"I don't know, Hank."

"Tell her you're taking a class. You have a teacher."

"Even so."

"She knows you beat off, right?"

"Not like she does. You ought to see her vibrator. It's got to be eight inches long."

Not the best example on my part, perhaps.

"Anyway," she said. "Would you show me? I've never done it."

"Jake gives instruction the first night."

"I can't be there at night. I told you guys. I want you to come to the house and show me. I don't want to be embarrassed."

"All right. I'll be happy to. But what if Lauren comes in?"

"She won't. She's at work. But if she does, I'll tell her we're there to fuck."

Wouldn't want to tell her something embarrassing.

The waitress came with the check. She looked at me pointedly as she tore it off. "You take care of this little girl."

Little? She was bigger than I was.

"It's not how it looks," Jess said. "We're just buddies."

"Yeah. You watch out for them buddies, young lady."

I gave her a 30 percent tip. She put up with a lot.

We walked down Prospect to Jess's house and she let us in, stepped into the living room. It wasn't spotless, but had undergone a transformation. All the magazines had been picked up, the CDs. The beer cans were gone, ashtrays empty.

"This place isn't always a pigsty," she said.

"I'm impressed." The posters were still on the wall, of course.

"I figured we'd do it out here, since you're scared of the bedroom. Wait a minute." She walked to the bedroom and came out, blushing. "I bought one of these."

It was a meditation cushion. She'd have been less embarrassed with her roommate's vibrator.

"I'm not saying I'm going to use it. But at least I've got it. One more blip on the credit card."

I didn't want to know her credit card debt.

We sat in the living room for instruction. I've done it literally dozens of times, taking care of the new students up in Maine, could have done it in my sleep. I try to tailor it to the particular person.

The thing about Zen is that it's simple exactly where you

expect it to be complicated. The Japanese are obsessed with physical posture, put more emphasis on that than any other tradition. But when you've finally got the posture figured out, there's nothing more. Some people teach following the breathing, and we give that to beginners. Might even let them count their breaths. But all that finally falls away and you're just sitting.

Think not thinking, Dogen said. *How do you think not thinking? Beyond thinking.* Figure that out.

"That's it?" Jess asked.

"The point is to do nothing," I said.

"You think this is what my mother did?"

"There are other ways to begin. But for most traditions, this is what it comes down to."

"Seems easy."

"Right. Nothing to it."

The instructions were simplicity itself, but what happened afterward could get complicated. The human mind is intricate.

"It doesn't quite, exactly, feel right," Jess said.

"You're leaning forward a little."

"I feel like I'm straight."

"You're pretty good. But you want to throw your shoulders back a little, puff out your stomach. I'll show you."

I moved behind Jess to adjust her posture, slid my hand up her spine, gently pulled her shoulders back, then reached around and touched her breasts.

"Oh Christ," I said.

It had been a problem, just a slight problem, that her skirt was so short, her legs white and bare. She wore that same light scent as the day before, and her hair smelled marvelous. Her shoulders were soft, and my hands seemed to move on their own. "I'm sorry, Jess. Jesus Christ. I didn't mean to do that."

She'd reddened, also smiled. "Maybe you did."

"No. It just happened."

"Maybe your hands know what you really want."

Maybe they did. That was why I didn't normally adjust women's posture during instruction.

"Why don't we see if they want to again?" she said.

I had moved in front of her, and she took my hands, put them on her breasts. I took them away.

"You want to fuck me," she said. "I know you do."

"I do."

"And I want you to. Really."

"I can't."

"What's wrong?"

"There's nothing wrong. But this is something else. I'm your teacher."

"So what? I fucked one of my teachers in high school."

Good grief. "He shouldn't have done that."

"He just should have done it better. Listen, Hank. Forget about it. You didn't show me anything."

"What?"

"I could have figured this much on my own. Sit there with my legs crossed."

"I suppose."

"So you're not my teacher. We really didn't do anything. You can fuck me."

I had moved away, but not too far. I didn't want her to take my hands again. She was smiling, flushed with passion.

"You don't understand," I said.

"Explain it to me."

I stood up, stepped over to a bean bag chair and sat. It would have helped if there had been some real furniture in the place.

"You're coming to the retreat on Friday," I said.

"Saturday. I've told you a million times. I can't come at night."

"Okay, Saturday."

"And I'm only going to stay a few hours. Can't stay long. I can't get up too early."

"Just be there at ten thirty. That's when Jake gives a talk. So you're becoming Jake's student. Even if it's only for a while. But that's the way everybody starts."

"All right."

"When you're Jake's student you're mine. I'm an extension of him." That was a stretch, but it seemed truer than it had a few days before. "And it's not appropriate to have sex with students. It's a violation."

"All right. I get it. So how do you get your rocks off?"

I shrugged. "Not everybody's a student."

"A lot of them must be. The women you meet. You're not tempted?"

"I'm tempted right now. Why do you think I'm sitting over here?"

She started up from her cushion.

"Sit down, Jess."

She sat back down, blushing. "This is still vaguely insulting."

"It's not meant that way. I'm telling you I want to. I'm just not going to."

"How about if I don't go to the retreat? Drop the whole thing?"

I shook my head. "You asked about it, Jess. You expressed a wish. You're Jake's student for life."

It was a strange thing to say, and Jess wrinkled her brow, but I honestly halfway believed it. There was a karmic tie.

And there was a rock-bottom notion in Zen that once you started on the path, you never got off. You could neglect it all you wanted, quit altogether. You were still there.

"You just beat off, don't you?" she said.

I shrugged. "A lot of the time."

"Me too," she said.

"Your roommate too."

She laughed.

"I kind of get it," she said. "I really do. But for me, I meet a nice guy. I mean, I was just trying to get the rent money. But then this guy takes me to breakfast. He takes me again. He talks to me about things that matter. He's not all over me. Doesn't go on and on about himself. He's old enough to be my grandfather, but what the hell. I'm not used to it. It's nice. So I want to fuck him. I don't see what's wrong."

That speech was the most persuasive thing she'd done. Even more than putting my hands on her breasts.

"There's nothing wrong," I said.

"And you're not going to do it," she said.

"Right."

"I don't see how you do this. I don't see why you do it. Taking me out. Being so nice."

"I once knew this guy who was a vegetarian," I said. "I'm not and neither is Jake, though a lot of Buddhists are. We were walking by this barbecue place, ribs and chicken, and the smell was overwhelming. Probably half their customers came in because of the smell. They must have wafted it out or something. I said to the guy, 'Don't you like that smell?'

"He said, 'Yes, it's great.'

"'Don't you want to go in?' I asked.

"He said, 'No. I've decided not to go in and I don't go in. I like the smell, but I don't go in. They're two different things.'"

"All right," she said. "At least you like my smell."

And a hell of a lot more than that.

"What do you do now?" she asked.

"I don't know. Probably take a swim at the Y. Jake's off with his sponsor."

"You think he fucks her?"

"Please, Jess. Enough."

"I bet she wants him to. I'm going to ask, when she sends me to art school."

She stood up, smoothed down her skirt.

"I'll walk you down," she said. "It's my day to go early and set up."

"You're going like that?"

"I'll come back and change. We've got to be black and tight at work. Short skirts and lots of cleavage. Get all the barflies hot and thirsty."

I figured it was a policy.

We walked out and headed down Prospect.

"So what are my chances of getting together with your little boy?" she asked. "If I can't have his daddy."

"I don't know, Jess. I'm seeing him tomorrow. I'll tell him where you work. Say his name came up and you like his column. He'll like that."

"Me and about a million other girls with big soft tits, I'm sure."

Jess did have a way of putting things.

"He doesn't come to meditation?" she asked.

"He likes Jake, but never wanted to meditate. Thinks I'm a little nuts."

"You are a little nuts. But you're okay."

We had crossed Mass. Ave., were standing on the corner.

"Tonight," I said, "when we come to the bar, tell me what hours you're coming to the retreat. Tell me like we haven't talked about it before. Jake doesn't know we're meeting."

"And why is that?"

"I don't know. I just haven't told him."

I wasn't sure why. Maybe I felt guilty, not absolutely sure I could hold out. Maybe I figured he'd think the whole thing unwise.

"It's because he'll think you're banging me," she said.

"No."

"He knows what a horny bastard you are." She wore a big smile. She really was a lovely woman without all the make-up, and the metal.

"Want to have breakfast tomorrow?" I asked.

"You like to torture yourself," she said.

"I just like having breakfast."

"All right, Hank. We'll do it." She took me by the shoulders and kissed me hard on the mouth. "Have a good swim. I hope the water's cold."

I hoped so too.

I turned toward the Y and saw Jake, about a block down. It was so unexpected, so much as if Jess had conjured him with words, so much the one person I didn't want to see, that for a moment I thought it was an apparition, my guilty conscience projecting him. What was worse was that he looked stricken, as if he'd just seen the worst thing he could possibly imagine. Rarely had I seen his face so abashed. He was walking straight at me, slowly. I waited for him to say something. Then I realized he was going to walk right past.

"Jake," I said. "What are you doing?"

"What?"

"What are you doing? Where are you going?"

"Just down here."

He nodded in the direction he was walking, his voice weak and distant.

"Don't you want to go this way?" I turned him around.

He didn't say anything.

"Why don't we go back to the Y? Maybe take a nap. Have you had lunch? I thought you were having lunch with Madeleine."

"Madeleine?"

"I thought you two were having lunch at one of those fancy restaurants."

We walked to the Y. There were four or five guys on the steps, hanging around the way they did, and they said, "Hey, Jake. How's it going, brother." One of them banged fists with him, like a basketball player. We went up to his room and got him to bed—that tape with his name was still on the door, but

I wasn't sure he even remembered it—lying face up. His face had calmed, didn't look so bewildered anymore, but he still didn't seem quite with me, stared up at the ceiling.

I sat beside him, on the floor, took his cushion and sat *zazen*. I don't know how he used that thing. It had no oomph at all.

I don't know how long I sat. It didn't seem terribly long, though it seemed a long time for him to be out that way.

Finally he said, "All right, I remember."

"What?"

"I spent the morning with Madeleine. We were going to have lunch. Then something came up and she had to meet somebody. She brought me back and dropped me off, and I stood with those guys on the steps talking."

I suppose he would have come back to himself sooner or later. I wondered where he might have wound up.

"So you haven't had lunch," I said.

"I haven't."

"Are you hungry?"

"Always." He sat up on the side of the bed, the old smile on his face. "What are you in the mood for?"

12

THE THING I LIKE about the Mexican place near Central Square is that it's not like the American idea of Mexican. Blazing hot salsas and gobs of cheese on everything, Corona beer with a lime on the top. It just had fresh ingredients and the best limeade I've ever tasted. People from all over the square come there.

Jake and I got one of the booths, so we could take our time.

It was only the purest accident that I'd shown up at Mass. Ave. when I had. Jake would have come to himself sooner or later, but who knows where he would have been, how many streets he would have crossed? I couldn't let him off by himself at all. If I wasn't with him, Madeleine had to be.

"That was bad, Jake," I said, early in the lunch.

"I really lost it." He was wearing that little smile.

"I haven't seen you like that."

"You just haven't noticed. Around the shop."

I didn't know how far gone he was sometimes.

"Maybe we can put a little collar on me," he said. "Like a dog."

He didn't see how serious this was.

"I'd have figured it out sooner or later," he said. "People would help me."

He was digging into his lunch, quesadillas with chicken and guacamole, corn chips on the side. It was a tad sloppy, squirting all over the place, but he sopped up the guacamole with his tortillas, went back for more limeade. There was nothing wrong with his appetite.

"Before I go completely gaga," he said after a while, "there's something I want to tell you."

"You're not going gaga," I said. "You just had a bad episode."

"Partly because I want to tell somebody. Partly because you need to hear it, if you're going to teach."

"I've been thinking about that. Don't know that I'm ready."

"You're never ready. You just do it, when the time comes."

I knew he was right. I couldn't picture it.

"Do you remember Olivia?" he asked.

Olivia. I drew a complete blank.

"She was with the group when you started. Years ago."

The group had been tiny. I thought I remembered everyone.

"That first summer, when you came just a time or two."

Jake couldn't remember who or where he was half the time, but was sure of something that happened twenty years before.

"Dark woman. Olive complexion. Big breasts."

Sounded like someone I would have noticed.

"You wouldn't have called her beautiful. Maybe not even pretty. But there was something about her. The one student I ever had who took to practice naturally. It isn't natural in a way. Goes against the habits of a lifetime. But if I ever had a student who dove right into it, it was her."

There was something different about the way Jake spoke to me now. He'd finished eating, we both had, but it was as if everything had stopped. There was a major pause in the middle of the room. He wasn't solemn, but didn't wear that little smile. He was just talking.

"If I'd had to pick a dharma heir, not that I was thinking of that then, it would have been her."

An odd thing to say to the person you'd just named your dharma heir two days before.

"She didn't feel like an equal. More like a superior. Naturally calm and still."

He seemed to gaze back on that time, looking down at his hands, one lying on top of the other on the table.

"Calm and still aren't everything, of course. But they're impressive."

He looked up and his gaze was entirely blank. It happened that quickly, like losing your place in a book, but more than that, as if the book disappeared. You didn't remember what reading was.

I waited a while, then put a hand on top of his. "Olivia," I said. "Twenty years ago. Your dharma heir."

He frowned. "That would have been a mistake." He contradicted himself from just seconds before. "It's better to have someone who struggled, who understands student struggles. It's better to have you."

It was *good* I was so screwed up.

"What happened to her?" I asked.

She had gone on to some other teacher? Contracted some terrible disease? Died?

"We became lovers. That's what I've been wanting to tell you."

For the first moment since it had happened, I wondered if he'd seen me with Jess that morning. I wondered if that was the incident that set him off, if it worked that way. I almost asked.

"I've been wanting to tell you for years," he said.

"Why didn't you?"

"The time wasn't right. You had that whole thing about sex. I didn't want to lecture."

"It isn't lecturing."

"Maybe I didn't want you to know. Who knows?"

"Christ, Jake. One woman. Compared to things I did."

I was lucky to keep it to one a day sometimes.

"I understood about not taking advantage of Madeleine. Who seemed to need me, really wanted me. Olivia didn't need me at all. Didn't have that yearning. She was my star."

I'd never heard him talk about anyone that way.

"That was what made her attractive," he said.

"So what happened?"

"At first it was amazing. The kind of connection you never have. She moved up in the off season and stayed for a while. We had a life together. A life of practice."

He heaved a big sigh, stared down at his hands.

"Then she got pregnant and wanted to have the child. I hesitated, and she noticed. I wasn't much of a breadwinner at the time."

"She had an abortion?"

"She had the child. Just wouldn't have anything more to do with me. I never saw her again."

He went through that right before I became his student. I'd had no idea.

Jake wasn't actively sad, but I'd never seen him so serious. He was making a point of telling me.

"It sounds as if I can't get involved with anyone," I said. "Might as well join a monastery."

"No. But when the person is a student, no matter how much it seems personal, it's always the dharma. That's what she's in love with."

I'd thought it was Jake all the women loved.

"It's natural to love the person who shows you that," he said. "Also natural to love your students. Talk to Socrates about that. But as soon as it gets physical, it becomes the old human mess. Which is wonderful. But bound to be a little disappointing, when she thought you were the Buddha."

I shook my head.

"Not literally," he said. "But that's where the confusion is."

People did idolize their teachers. I'd seen it a million times.

"So what do you do about all this?" I asked. "Sex. Women."

"Find somebody who's not the least bit interested. Thinks meditation is stupid. Remember Ethel?"

Ethel had been a chunky little waitress at the downtown diner near the bike shop. I'd seen her fawn all over Jake, hadn't thought much of it. She'd died five or six years ago.

"You don't mean it," I said.

"She was a Catholic. Thought I was going straight to hell. Maybe that made it exciting."

"She didn't want to get married?"

"She'd been married. Besides. Who in their right mind marries a part-time bicycle repairman?"

In the grand Mexican tradition, the one dessert the place had was flan. Jake had some, though I didn't think it was sweet enough. I drank some coffee. We strolled back out onto Mass. Ave. toward the Y.

"So what happened to Olivia? Do you ever wonder?"

"All the time. Madeleine kept me posted. She kept track of her."

"She never wanted to see you?"

"Wouldn't even talk about me, at least to Madeleine. There was some deep problem. I never understood. Maybe that's why the old monks were celibate. There's deep wisdom in that."

Jake didn't look sad, or upset. He did look tired. It had taken a toll on him, telling me. I wondered why he had picked that moment.

"I'm ready for a nap," he said.

We went up to the rooms. That hallway was never too bright, with its off-green institutional walls, dull lighting. There was something depressing about it, with the stale smell.

"I'm going to read afterward," Jake said.

"I'll take a swim. Come back after that."

There was something I needed to bring up, wasn't sure how. I settled on bluntness. "Don't go wandering off," I said.

"I'll have my clothes off," he said. "I'm not that dotty."

"You'll stay in your room."

"I'm not going to piss in the sink, if that's what you mean."

"Just leave your door open."

It was only for a minute or two.

"I'll be in here or down at the pool," I said.

I didn't take a nap, just lay on my back and pondered things. That wasn't a bombshell, exactly, but definitely some new information about the man who had been the biggest influence on my life.

In the brief history of American Zen there have been various sex scandals, mostly Japanese teachers coming to this country and fucking their brains out. The situation has been analyzed to death, the comparison with incestuous dysfunctional families definitely covered. People got quite exercised about it.

The truth seemed to be that the priests—they weren't celibate; Zen priests can marry—were men who fell into a situation where women worshipped them. Not surprisingly, they found that hard to resist. The women who wound up in zendos seemed prone to such situations, also prone to outrage about them. The whole thing was a mess.

All I had was Jake's side of the story of his relationship with Olivia, but this didn't sound like that. Jake hadn't preyed on a weak person. It was a meeting of equals.

The great teachers through history were solitaries. Jesus, the Buddha, almost anyone you wanted to name—Lao-tzu riding off to be a hermit when someone made him write the *Tao Te Ching*—devoted themselves not to family life but to something else. If you want to know if you're enlightened, people used to say, ask your wife. These men didn't have wives.

Maybe that's why we think they were enlightened.

I had long since stopped thinking Jake was perfect. It was because he was so human that I admired him: he had taken the raw materials of humanity and made something wonderful, with no tool other than sitting and watching it all, learning to accept.

After about an hour I took a swim. I hadn't heard any stirring next door at all. There were four of us in the pool, but I had my own lane. That goofy pool was starting to grow on me.

Often, swimming brings up something altogether new. It's a kind of Zen activity. Strange to say, but it hasn't been my experience that thoughts reside in the brain. They permeate the body, as does the mind (which is different from the brain). "Everything is mind" is the famous Zen saying, but that doesn't mean, as people think, that everything is all in your head. It means your mind is your body. It's also the grass, the trees, the birds singing outside.

Anyway, that act of swimming changed my mind. By the time I finished, I thought the real issue was Jess. In the grand scheme of things she was like Madeleine more than like Olivia, a confused, needy person looking for help. It was only the sheerest accident that we walked into the bar and she heard about the retreat, but everything was like that: I happened into a bike shop twenty years before and saw a flyer about Zen classes. I hadn't been looking.

I met Jake and knew he had something I wanted. She seemed to do the same. A dozen barflies heard we were having that retreat, and they didn't express interest. Jess didn't really care about art school, didn't want to go to that class in the fall, but she did want to meditate. Scared shitless, but she wanted to learn.

She also wanted to fuck me. And that would ruin everything.

It wasn't really me. She'd just happened to meet a couple of older guys who weren't treating her as a slutty bar girl. She wanted to know them, tried to do so in the usual way. Which turned her right back into a slutty bar girl. She tried to get away from that and walked right into it.

121

I—when I was being truthful—would have loved to do what she wanted. There was nothing I'd have liked more than to go back to that bedroom. That was what I'd face for the rest of my life if I did this. One woman after another like Jess.

I took a shower and went upstairs, hesitated a moment, knocked on Jake's door. He was sitting in bed reading, his little reading spectacles down on his nose.

"I went out and wandered aimlessly for a while, like a lunatic," he said. "Now I'm back."

He was reading the Shobogenzo, the great lifetime work of our Zen lineage's founding teacher, from the thirteenth century.

"How's the book?" I said.

"As you lose your mind, it almost makes sense."

We got together again when we headed for the bar. The sun was setting red over the buildings. Traffic had slowed. I could almost imagine living in that city.

I asked Jake the one question that really bothered me, about that man who seemed to notice every detail.

"How'd you let her get pregnant?" I asked.

"You still carrying her around?" he asked.

"I am. And she's heavy, being pregnant and all."

"Of all the phrases in the history of romance, the least romantic is, 'Is your diaphragm in?' Night after night that phrase spoils things a little. Night after night, because you've just gotten together, the answer is yes. There's one night you don't ask. That's the night you should have."

The Green Street Grill for some reason was a total madhouse that evening, whether we were arriving late or what. The regulars were there somewhere, a few turned and bowed, but were buried in a crowd three and four deep at the bar, waiting for the restaurant. This was what I'd heard the place was like. We must have come on off nights.

We didn't get our central seats at the bar, didn't get any. We were lucky to get to the bar, which took five minutes and a major effort. Jess had a couple of women helping her. As soon as she saw us, she poured our beer and came over. We stood at the far side, where the crowd had finally thinned out. She leaned over and took Jake's face in her hands, kissed his cheek.

"Hi, Padre," she said. "This place is a zoo."

"You said it."

"Everybody wants a drink *now*. Two drinks, in case they can't get me later. If they don't get a drink they'll slit their throats."

People got frantic when their alcohol was threatened.

"Anyway," she said. "Fuck 'em. How are you?"

She looked different, I can't say how. She was back in uniform, had the short tight skirt that looked as if her ass were about to burst through like a blooming flower, the tight top showing major cleavage. She had the earrings, the nose ring. I could have sworn the hair streaks were heading in the blond direction, but maybe it was just the light.

But she still had something of the girlish quality from that morning. It was as if she were dressed up in a costume.

"I'm fine," Jake said. "A few senior moments today." Major understatement. "But feeling good."

"You look adorable."

Jake actually blushed.

"Do I have to stand on my head to get a drink around here?" a guy down the bar said.

"You might try it," Jess said. "Why don't you do that? You've had three that I know of."

"I don't ask you to count my drinks. Just bring them."

"I'm talking to my priest, cocksucker. Learn some manners."

Jake took a slug of his beer.

"I'm sorry, Padre," Jess said. "Where were we?"

"Telling him he's adorable," I said.

"I talked to my friend again," Jake said. "She'll see you at the retreat. Looking into art class options."

123

"Honestly, Padre. It was a girlish whim."

"She's just a helpful person. Have you figured out when you're coming?"

"I'm thinking around ten. Stay until four."

"Nine fifty would be better," I said. "We start a sitting then."

"You get there when you can," Jake said. "We'll fit you in."

"I can make nine fifty," she said.

"You don't want to miss Hank's talk," Jake said.

Christ. He had eliminated himself altogether.

He handed her a slip of paper with the address.

"I'll be there with bells on," she said. "But I've got to go. The drunkards of the world await."

She leaned over and kissed him again, pinched his cheek.

"You're so cute," she said.

Jake downed the rest of his Guinness in one gulp. A little tough to pace myself with that.

"This place is obnoxious tonight," he said. "Let's go."

I had to put my beer down the same way. About five minutes later it hit me like a hammer.

Further down Mass. Ave. than we usually went, halfway to Harvard Square, was a little place that made Italian sandwiches. They baked the thin crusty loaves of bread on the premises, filled them with prosciutto, mozzarella, fresh tomatoes, basil. The place was packed at lunch, not bad in the evening. After Green Street we needed some quiet.

"She's going to come not knowing how to meditate," Jake said. "You'll give her instruction."

"I'll take care of it."

That was the time, if there ever was one, to tell Jake about already giving her instruction, seeing her for breakfast the last two days, but I couldn't get past the fact that I'd grabbed her boobs. I felt guilty.

"She may have trouble," he said. "Seems a little squirmy."

"It'll work out."

You never knew how *sesshin* would be for somebody new, even somebody old. It was a total crapshoot.

We ate for a while. There was nothing like that fresh-baked bread.

"This Olivia," I said. "Was she the love of your life?'

He shrugged, gazed down at his plate.

"I assume not Ethel," I said.

I couldn't say how many times that woman had brought me a plate of pancakes as I sat right beside Jake, never suspecting. That was as much a bombshell as the other news.

"Ethel came closer, if I'm being honest. Didn't ask a lot of life or of me. Never even cared if I spent the night, since I got up so early. I haven't met many like her."

I haven't met any. She was the last person I'd have put Jake with.

"Olivia was different." He put down his sandwich, took a drink of his beer. He was having two that night. "For one thing, I knew her such a short time. Five months. Then not to know her at all, even to see her, for twenty-some years."

In a way, Jake said, he hadn't known much about her. She showed up in his class at the beginning of the summer. She was a little on the countercultural side, wore peasant blouses and blue jeans, maybe a T-shirt when it was really hot. She was a major athlete and outdoorswoman, rode a bike all over the island, went canoeing and waterskiing, jogged. She'd done modern dance when she was younger, was very physical.

"I think that's why she got into it so quickly," he said. "Sometimes when you've practiced a discipline like dance it comes naturally. Sitting is physical."

As he'd spent the last twenty years telling me.

"How old was she?" I asked.

"Your age. Madeleine's. I can't believe you don't remember."

I didn't think I'd ever seen her.

She was something of a mysterious person, he said, a private person. There were aspects of her life—her parents and family—she didn't talk about at all. He didn't know how she was able to be up there all summer, so casually move up for the fall. She said she was in transition, used that expression a lot, but didn't say why. She didn't like him asking.

"I had the idea something had happened," he said. "Some major life change. But she never said a word."

Most people would have told their meditation teacher, to say nothing of their boyfriend.

"But I never in my life saw someone get into meditation so fast. We had three all-days that summer and they weren't a problem. At the beginning of the fall we did a five-day and she breezed through that. It was as if she already knew what the whole thing was about. If there was ever an argument for past lives, it was someone like her. Who seemed to know practice when she got here."

I had an uncle who believed in reincarnation when he saw Art Tatum play the piano. "No way he could have learned that in one lifetime," he said. "Impossible."

"And I want to tell you, Hank. Which is why I mentioned it. Having sex with that woman was the most natural thing in the world. Our minds had been in the same place, as if we were the same person. Sex didn't seem to make it different. She moved in soon after. I thought we'd teach together some-day. It made sense to have a woman assistant, with so many women students."

By that time we had finished our dinners and the place had cleared out. They stayed open until nine.

"She got pregnant and it changed everything. She'd have the baby and find a way to raise it. I agreed that was the thing to do. I just couldn't see how. Came to a block in the road and hesitated. A classic Zen moment, in a way. Suddenly she was the teacher and I the struggling student."

He shook his head.

"She blew through the roadblock and took off. I'd flunked the koan."

I needed to meet this woman. I wasn't sure I'd like her, but I'd like to meet her.

"I don't get the bitterness," I said.

"What?"

"Never seeing you again. Not letting you see the child. That should ease up after a while."

I wasn't best friends with my ex-wife, but we got along.

"I wrote her letters through the years, sent them through Madeleine. Never heard a word. It's one thing to get a hostile reception. Gives you something to work with. But nothing." He shook his head.

There was something weird about that, verging on pathological. She might have impressed Jake in some ways, but she had something to learn about compassion. It would have helped the child to know his father. Especially a father as loving as Jake.

This was one of those unenlightened restaurants—as far as Jake was concerned—that didn't see dessert as the crowning moment of the meal. There wasn't a whole lot to be had at that hour out on Mass. Ave., lots of bars but not an abundance of coffee houses. We finally found one up across from the Y, a funky place that seemed eclectic, aging hippies reading discarded newspapers but also kids tapping away at their laptops, text messaging on their cell phones, checking their pagers, whatever they do. It's all beyond me.

We managed to hook Jake up with a big crumbly chocolate cookie, a small cup of coffee, got him into bed not too long after that, curled up with his Buddhist sutras. One more night at the Y and we moved to our new digs.

13

THE GOLDEN D that last morning had a muffin I'd never run into before, blueberry corn. "Only on Friday," Lily said. "One day we serve this muffin."

"Why is that?"

"People come for fish cakes and beans Friday. This muffin give them special treat."

I gazed at Jake. "Catholics have been eating meat on Friday for years," I said.

"These old Cambridge neighborhoods are hardcore. Haven't given up."

Haul out the tuna noodle casserole.

Parts of Cambridge—a mile in either direction from Central Square—were on the cutting edge of the twenty-first century, but Cambridgeport seemed a throwback. Matrons in house-dresses out sweeping the sidewalks, broad-faced Irishmen off to work in the morning with lunch buckets, neighborhood characters still walking the streets talking to themselves. Other cultures had spiced the place up—a Jamaican market, Indian grocery—but the originals were still there.

This muffin in any case was a brilliant invention, tart little berries finding a perfect home in dense, grainy cornbread. Along with their superb coffee and (alas) a tiny glass of Minute Maid orange juice, it made an excellent breakfast.

Jake was still eating eggs but had the special muffin too. He liked a hearty breakfast.

Lily stepped over. "What you eat at these retreats?" she asked. "Who do the cooking?"

I hoped this wasn't her way of telling us the Golden Donut catered.

"The Japanese eat rice and pickled vegetables," Jake said. "We have a soup and salad at lunch. Rice and vegetables at night. Oatmeal in the morning."

Meals in the zendo were ceremonial, people coming in to serve us as we sat on our cushions. The bowls were small, but you didn't need much food just for sitting.

"The cook is the most important person in a Japanese temple," Jake said. "A senior monk."

"Food most important thing," Lily said.

In our case Madeleine's cook, Darcy, would be the senior monk. Her only problem would be keeping it from being too good. Food should be simple and bland, not a distraction. You didn't want people to focus on it.

A soup of poor greens, Dogen said, *was as important as a cream soup for the emperor.*

"You want maybe put out donuts in the morning? Give people treat?"

I would like to think—and dearly hope—that Jake only considered this suggestion to be nice. Didn't want to come down on Lily too hard.

"We serve a treat in the afternoon," he said.

In the late afternoon, when people's spirits and blood sugar flag, there was a ceremonial tea, along with a tea treat. It was one of my favorite moments of the day (you can be damn sure it was Jake's). It was a remarkable experience to bring the concentration of a retreat onto that one little cookie, a small cup of tea. It was how you should eat everything.

Double chocolate donuts would make the same point, but I wasn't sure how the late afternoon would go.

"We deliver donuts MIT every day," Lily said.

And those people were smart.

"Let me think about it," Jake said. "I'll get back to you."

I fully expected to see a donut in my breakfast bowl the first morning.

Before we left, without saying anything to me, Jake walked over and sat beside the scared woman in the overcoat. The omelet man wasn't there that day. In all the times we'd come to the Golden Donut, I hadn't seen any expression on that woman's face except deep anxiety, desperate to catch a bus that never showed up.

But Jake had a way with people. If he reminded me of any-one—others remarked on this too—it was the Chinese monk known as Hotei in Japan, the fat guy with a sack who has been made into a good luck charm. Supposedly there was such a man in ancient China, who pulled sweets out of his bag to give children but could also speak with monks and put them back on track with their practice.

Jake wasn't that fat (a few more weeks in Cambridge and he would be) but had that effect. He sat there talking for a few minutes and the woman actually smiled. A couple minutes more and Lily was over there taking her order, on Jake.

"Turned out she *was* hungry," he said, as he came back to me.

The whole world is hungry.

The donut of choice that day was a lemon jelly concoction, powdered sugar on the top. Jake always took Lily's sugges-tion, never seemed disappointed.

The weather had turned cold that morning, a slate gray sky, gusting winds. We wore our jackets, and Jake had on his beret. One of the things I liked most about New England was its extremes. You could go from balmy to bitterly cold within a few hours.

We were walking to Madeleine's to make final plans.

"You get nervous before *sesshin?*" Jake asked.

"Always." No matter how many times I'd done it. It always surprised me.

Though I had reason for nerves this time. The thought of those talks every day, no idea of the subject, loomed like a black hole.

"I used to have a friend," Jake said, "a teacher in Japan, who said good-bye to people before *sesshin* as if he might never see them again. Didn't know if he'd come out."

My grandmother used to tell me always to do that. Say good-bye every time as if it's the last. It may be.

"*Sesshin* is like death," Jake said.

It was that kind of dread.

On the one hand, it was a great relief to stop being yourself eighteen hours a day. That was hard work. At the same time, it was that abandonment of self that was so fearful. When you can't talk, can't write, can't read, give up everything that makes you you, who are you? It's terrifying.

"That's what I'll be talking about, if you want a little preview," Jake said.

I'd take any preview I could get.

"Death. It's what keeps coming up."

I'd noticed. Jake had always taken the subject lightly, made casual reference to it, but I'd never heard him mention his own death so much as in the past few days.

"Having this illness is like a preview. You keep falling into a hole. Like the time I was in a car accident when I was young and got amnesia. The strangest sensation. I came to on a hospital table and was clearly awake, looking around, but had no idea who I was."

"Good grief."

"That morning, it was funny, my girlfriend had given me bacon for breakfast. We almost never had bacon. But I had an aftertaste, lying there on that table. It was a little thread that pulled my whole life up."

Where does the memory go, when it isn't there? How can it come back?

"I'm not unhappy, Hank," he said.

It was one of the things I worried about the most, though he never seemed that way.

"It's scary, this illness. But I've been scared before. You fall into that hole and just watch things, let them be. I come back eventually, though I suppose there'll be a day when I don't. But it's not a bad place, if you live as we have. The person you really are is there. It's the small self that's disappeared."

I knew that was true theoretically. I didn't know how it felt.

"But if I stop making sense," he said. "If I'm still talking, but you can see I'm not there, you've got to step in."

"I will."

That assumed I'd know. Zen teachings in general don't always make much sense.

Madeleine looked thrilled when she came to the door; this day was the fruition of all her dreams, when she would finally have Jake teaching at this center she'd wanted for so long. She welcomed him effusively, actually went so far as to hug and kiss me. They went to the meditation hall to make sure it was the way he wanted. I went to the kitchen to see Darcy.

She was a small dumpy woman in her sixties, had worked for Madeleine for years. She had a round face that was deeply wrinkled, sad eyes that never looked my way, but was a no-nonsense woman who seemed totally in charge, had cooked huge dinner parties through the years, elaborate menus. A little oatmeal every morning wouldn't faze her.

"Jake talked to you about the meals," I said.

"He said it should be bean soup at lunch every day. It's not easy to cook seven bean soups. Make them all different."

Actually, according to Madeleine, she could have cooked thirty in a row. She was a wizard. But her eyes looked so sad I hardly knew what to say.

"It doesn't have to be bean," I said. "Just a hearty soup. The main meal."

"Plain rice at night," she said, looking forlorn. "Doesn't make much of a supper."

"You can jazz it up a little. Jake won't say so, but he'll like it."

"A hambone would help those soups."

"That we can't do. We've got some strict vegetarians."

"You hardly notice a little ham. It adds flavor."

"I'd love it myself. But some of these people would be horrified."

Jake had been over all this with Darcy. She said the same things every time.

"You can make a special dinner for me and Jake when it's all over. Cook the whole ham if you want."

"I will."

She walked around tidying up, touching her knives and various utensils. She was dying to get started. Wished we'd start right then.

"Plain oatmeal in the morning," she said. "You can make it so much better with maple syrup. Raisins and dates. He doesn't even want milk."

"If things show up in the oatmeal he'll have to eat them."

"I never heard of such a thing. No milk."

"Jazz it up a little. But please do skip that hambone. You'll have a bunch of hysterical lesbians out here."

For the first time she laughed. "We can't have that."

I walked back into the main part of the house, the meditation hall. Jake was sitting in his place, trying it out. You wouldn't have called his posture classic; he was a chunky little guy, and his torso just blobbed down on the cushion like a pile of mud. But beneath the robes he wore at *sesshin*—people didn't see—his legs were in full lotus, and he could sit that way forever and then stand up as if he hadn't been down. His legs were like rubber.

He seemed to have settled into sitting, Madeleine to one side. I motioned her out.

"You two having lunch today?" I asked.

"Darcy's fixing something. You're welcome to stay."

She said that, but I knew what she wanted.

"I've got plans. But we've got to hook up at the Y when you come back. Set a time."

I told her what had happened the day before, the way he'd wandered off.

"He told me he'd be fine," she said. "There were other men there. He joined right in."

Jake could blend in with any group, stand there and talk Red Sox baseball as if he were in the bleachers every day. He only read about it in the paper.

"They don't know to watch him," I said. "Don't know anything about him."

"I'm mortified. It was a last-minute thing."

"I'd have thought it was okay. Didn't think he'd wander. Why don't you show up around three. I'll wait on the steps."

Jake and I were having an early dinner with Josh since *sesshin* began at eight thirty. I'd had the bright idea earlier that morning to make it at Green Street, so Jess could meet him. Josh said he'd pay, which made the whole thing doable. He liked treating the old man, now that he had money.

"Jake told me about Olivia last night," I said to Madeleine.

"I thought you knew," she said.

"I never heard until yesterday."

"I thought you knew her in the old days. Would have gone after her. I mean, she was a woman."

"Jesus, Madeleine."

"Well?"

"You weren't just some woman to me."

She gave me her most skeptical frown.

I felt we were friends, as close as two people can be after a romance. The association with Jake helped.

"This is wonderful," I said, "what you're doing for Jake."

"I don't know why it's taken so long."

There was that question again: why had Jake, after all these years, decided finally to acquiesce and come to Cambridge? Just for me?

I didn't like that idea.

"It's a beautiful setup," I said.

"I hope things go well."

There was no way they could be too bad. Jake had a core of fifteen students whom he'd worked with for years and who knew the whole routine. There would be new people like Jess, but the veterans would take care of them. With a group together this long, a retreat ran itself.

"*Sesshins* scare me," she said.

She wore a look of real anxiety. The problem wasn't logistics.

"They scare everybody," I said.

It was the people who had trouble—the vast majority—who were the real Zen students. They were being brave.

"You two conspiring against me?" Jake suddenly appeared in the hall.

"You were deep in *samadhi*," I said. "We didn't want to disturb you."

"Taking a snooze," he said. "That's a nice room. Beautiful center."

"I agree," I said.

Madeleine was beaming. The fear had left her face.

She was someone who made practice available, rather than doing it herself.

"Don't overdo it at lunch," I said. "We're meeting Josh early."

"I'll be ready," Jake said.

"I'll meet you at the Y."

I looked at Madeleine, and she nodded.

It was an invigorating day for a walk. The wind was gusting, trees shaking and shedding their leaves. It didn't look like rain, just a cold cloudy day. I walked to Harvard Yard, cut through to Mass. Ave., made it to Inman Square a few minutes before I was supposed to meet Jess. But she was in the restaurant waiting for me, just like before.

I was glad she could be on time. She'd need to.

She seemed to be dressed for me, a purple blouse and white skirt this time (not too short, thank God), no makeup or jewelry. I was stunned at how different the effect was.

"You look great, Jess," I said.

"I feel like a job interview," she said. "Not my usual. I thought you might bring Padre."

Maybe that's who she was dressing for.

"I still haven't told him we have breakfast," I said.

"He saw me kiss you yesterday. He was just a block away."

That was the impression I'd had too; he couldn't have missed.

"I was just being sassy," she said. "Giving you a hard time. Then when I saw him I was so embarrassed. He didn't say anything?"

I explained about Jake's spells, that it had taken a while to bring him out of that one.

"He saw, believe me," Jess said. "He might not have known who we were, but he saw."

Our little waitress came and took our orders, brought coffee. The place was busier that morning, maybe two-thirds full.

"I tried meditating," she said. "Not a rousing success."

I smiled. "When?"

"Right before I came. I figured it would be this time tomorrow."

"Right."

"I don't know if I can do this. I wanted to, and I tried, but I don't know. I don't think I followed a single breath."

I gave her the usual speech for beginners. Following the

breath was a technique to let you see things. It didn't matter how you did. *Don't think good or bad*, Dogen said. *Don't judge right or wrong.* What was important was seeing your body and mind. The mind usually dominates.

"It really does," Jess said. "My God. I'm nuts."

"No more than anybody else."

"I can't believe my mother did this every day. Can't believe you do it."

"It's going to be different at retreat. People all around."

"What if I run from the room like a maniac?"

"It happens. The important thing is to show up. Come when you say you will. That's half the battle at least. More than half."

"How did you get started at this? How did Padre? I don't get this."

"It's different ways for different people."

"Like what?"

I figured I'd tell about Jake, what I knew. His was a far more interesting story than mine.

He had been an art student in the late fifties, out on the West Coast. Not a Beatnik exactly, but they influenced the atmosphere. He was too serious to identify with any movement. He really meant to devote his life to art.

He loved Asian art, Chinese and Japanese, decided on a whim in his early thirties to go to Japan. He didn't have a plan. A couple of years before he had hitchhiked around Europe, now he was heading for Asia. Something about that spare style, the use of space, appealed to him. He was a man with no particular responsibilities. He just took off.

He got a job teaching English, which was easy to find, also began studying Japanese, looking for an artist to study with. The man he found was like no other teacher he'd ever had, even allowing for cultural differences. He painted landscapes, and Jake loved his work, but before Jake could do anything the man made him sit and stare at landscapes by the hour. "You look," the man said. "Just look." It was most of the English he knew.

Jake also did lots of tasks like cleaning up, mixing paints, getting groceries; for a long time the man didn't let him do any painting. He had to learn to sit in front of the canvas, pick up the brush, take the proper posture. He also had to learn to sit. The day began with a period of *zazen*, though Jake didn't know what it was. "You just sit," the man would say, another big speech for him. They sat until the teacher let him get up.

Much of the communication was in the form of grunts, shoves, head-shaking, wordless shouts. The day began at dawn and was over by two; Jake taught his English lessons in the late afternoon and early evening. Finally, when he could communicate a little better, he asked about the sitting they were doing in the morning. The artist took him to his Zen teacher, a man named Kosho Uchiyama.

By the time he met Uchiyama he was starting to get the idea. He'd come to Japan as an ambitious artist, wanting to accomplish things, make a name for himself, but here the emphasis was on life before art: learning to keep the place neat and be humble before your teacher, learning to observe and appreciate the landscape before you did something so presumptuous as painting it. You had to learn to walk, learn to stand, learn to sit. For weeks and months he resisted, but finally he gave in. He sat and stared at the landscape by the hour. He came to love it.

Uchiyama was a disciple of a famously charismatic teacher named Kodo Sawaki, who had recently died. In the face of what they saw as widespread corruption in Zen—temples being passed down from father to son and existing primarily as places for weddings and funerals, monks who trained for a few years and then hardly sat again—they took over a ruined, abandoned temple and began to live as monks once had, living by begging, devoting themselves to sitting, doing retreats once a month. For years they only had a few adherents, but over time the sincerity of their practice drew attention.

The basic teaching of the founder of their school—the thirteenth-century monk named Dogen Zenji—was that the whole of the Buddha's teaching is expressed through *zazen*. Dogen had traveled to China to find a true teacher, and when he came back to Japan—in his late twenties—wrote a famous small text recommending *zazen* to all people, not just monks. His most stunning piece of writing—a three-page piece called the "Genjokoan"—was a letter to a layman. Eventually he became more of a monastic, but Sawaki and Uchiyama took his teaching seriously. The heart of what they did was *zazen*, and everyone was welcome.

They had brutal *sesshins* once a month, much more sitting than we do, and the first one Jake did was a turning point. He thought by that time that he had changed his attitude toward everything, but really he'd just transferred his ambitions from art to spiritual practice. He went to that *sesshin* with the goal of mastering *zazen*.

By the third day he was in agony. His body ached and was tied up in knots. He sat with tears rolling down his cheeks. He had failed at painting—he was thirty-some years old and was a glorified janitor for some eccentric Japanese—and now he was failing at this. He couldn't even sit and stare at the wall. He actually stood up from his place and walked out. Uchiyama didn't do anything.

"You can do that?" Jess asked. "Just leave?"

"Who's going to stop you?" I said.

"I thought they hit you with a stick."

"No sticks for Uchiyama. No talks. No nothing. You just sat."

Jake walked around the city, still breaking into sobs from time to time, he was so frustrated. The practice seemed simple, but he couldn't do it. He couldn't do the simplest thing.

Somehow, at the same time—this made no logical sense—he could see that there was nothing in the world to do but *zazen*. He had no recourse. He walked around for an hour, went back to the temple, and took his place again. Uchiyama still didn't say anything. He never spoke of the incident at all.

Jake wound up staying for twelve years. Uchiyama had a saying, "Sit for ten years. Then sit another ten. Then sit another ten," so there was no satisfying the man. Jake returned to this country an ordained Zen priest from an extremely austere tradition; that and ninety-five cents bought him a cup of coffee. He traveled around trying to find a place to practice, but nothing seemed right. "Probably I was proud," he said. "I had a bug up my ass when I got back here." The last place he tried, having traveled across the country, was in Maine. When that didn't work out he went to Mount Desert Island and worked as a limo driver, short-order cook, bicycle repairman. He was the kind of person who was good at most things.

"He gave up art?" Jess asked.

"He still did some sketching and painting, as a way of appreciating the world. He had no ambition."

After a while, in Bar Harbor, he began to give meditation classes in the tourist season. He felt he was good at basic instruction and that people could profit from the classes. He didn't have great plans, but over the years he developed a following, and things grew from there.

"The same thing happened with you, when you met him," Jess said.

"Not as dramatically, but yes, over time. I started doing it for myself, had other work altogether. After a while nothing else seemed as important."

Jess leaned back and stretched, gave a big yawn. We had demolished our breakfast, were sitting over coffee.

"That's not going to happen to me," she said.

"No reason it should. It can be important and not be your whole life. I could go back to something else."

Until recently, I'd thought I'd probably teach high school again after Jake died.

"Look at your mother," I said. "It was important to her."

"I used to get mad when I was a teenager. It was part of what I resented. The way she was so perfect about everything. But she still did it when she was quite sick. Not the yoga, but the meditation. I wish I could ask her about it."

She smiled, shaking her head, but there were tears in her eyes.

"One time right toward the end, she said, 'This shows me where I'm going.'"

The woman must have gone deep.

"Anyway," Jess said. "I'm scared now. Scared shitless."

"You're just going to sit," I said. "You can always leave."

"What if I can't do it?"

"There's actually nothing to do. You want to remember that."

"But what if I can't take it? You don't know how nuts I am."

"Believe me, Jess. I've been as nuts as anyone. I know how it is."

"What do you think he meant, there's nothing to do but *zazen?* There's lots of things. Drinking. Listening to music. Fucking."

"What he meant was that you've got to look at yourself. Sooner or later you've got to look. Pay attention. You can spend your life running from it, but that's a form of suffering. You think you want to run, it makes everything easier, but it's easier to face it. That's the weird part. When you finally sit down to face it, and that might take years, it's easy. Much easier than what you've been doing."

Jess shook her head. "Sometimes I wish I'd never heard of this. You guys had never walked into the bar. Of all the gin joints in all the world."

141

"We had to walk into yours. It was your karma."

I had paid the check and we stood from our seats.

"It might be easy," I said. "It might be absolutely nothing. You don't know."

Sometimes, when someone got their nervousness out before they began, the whole thing was easier than they thought.

On our way back to her apartment, I told her we were going to have dinner at Green Street that night, with Josh.

"No shit," she said. "The famous Josh Wilder at my bar."

"If he can get a seat."

"Friday nights are the worst."

"We're coming early. Five-thirty. We have to get back to start *sesshin*."

"That shouldn't be bad. The drunks will be there, but the dinner crowd comes later."

We had reached her corner, turned and headed to her place.

"I can't believe that tomorrow at this time I'm going to be sitting there staring at a wall. For four fucking hours or something."

"There's going to be a talk after your first sitting," I said. "Lunch, and a work break. You won't be sitting that much."

"Quite a bit for a person who can't do it at all."

"You can reduce the time you stay. Adjust as you go along. You don't want to push too hard."

We didn't usually give someone so many outs, but it was unusual to have someone who hadn't sat at all. I didn't know why Jake encouraged her.

We walked through the doorway, were just inside the living room, taking off our jackets. She tossed mine on a chair, put hers in the closet. The place still looked neat.

"Oh *Christ*," she said. "I'm getting all jittery again. I'm going to have to smoke dope or something. Does anybody do that?"

"No, Jess. Despite the prevailing rumors. Dope smoking and Zen do not go hand in hand."

"Give me a hug, Hank. I swear to God I'm going to keel over. My *knees* are shaking."

She put her arms around my shoulders and practically collapsed. I got my arms around her and gave a big squeeze, held her tight. Her body really was trembling. We stood a few moments, waiting for her to calm down.

She leaned back and looked at me. "Let's fuck," she said. She leaned forward and gave me a long wet kiss.

I kissed her, I admit it. It had been a while since I'd kissed anyone and I suppose I saw it coming. In any case, I did do it, stood there kissing her for quite a while. My cock jumped— I was pleased to see it could be so quick—and she pressed against me. I let the kiss go on. She finally pulled away.

"Fuck me," she said. "I can tell you want to." She reached down and grabbed it.

"I do, but I'm not going to."

"You've got to. You're so hard. Look at you. You're a hypo- crite."

"I'm not a hypocrite. I admit I want to. I'm just not doing it."

"I need it. I'm about to go nuts here. I need a man inside me. Please, Hank."

"Jess. You might need a man. I'm sure you've got lots of men. And your roommate's got that vibrator in her bedroom. There's a lot you can do."

"That won't cut it. I *know*. I need a man to go through me."

"Tomorrow I'm going to be talking to you. Or the next day. Or the next. I'm going to be your meditation teacher, and I'm going to be helping you with things that come up. If we fuck, the whole thing will be fucked. You won't listen to me.

"What we're going to do is much more important than sex. Sex is just a way to get away from it, one of the millions of ways people have. But you can't get away. We've got to stay with it. This is the beginning of that. The retreat begins now."

"Maybe I won't do it."

"The retreat began days ago. We're way into it. It began when you decided to sign up."

I removed her hand from my cock, which she'd been clutching the whole time. A few more minutes of that and the whole thing would be a moot point.

"I don't know what you're talking about," she said. "But if you can stand there with your dick hard in my hand and still don't want me, the hell with you. Go."

I picked up my jacket.

"It was a good kiss," she said.

"It was a great kiss," I said.

"This is your last chance to fuck a twenty-year-old chick in your whole life, and you're turning it down. You pathetic old fart."

Life did have its little ironies.

"You're a beautiful woman, Jess," I said, "an amazing woman, and you're going to be at that retreat tomorrow. I'm going to see you."

"Don't count on it."

"It'll be the first of many times. We're going to know each other for years."

I didn't know where that came from.

I opened the door, stepped out, and closed it behind me. That was a close fucking call. One more kiss and I was a goner.

I looked around as if I'd just reentered the world, stretched and heaved a huge sigh. A woman across the way was sweeping her steps. Traffic roared by on Prospect. Starting that evening, for the next five days, I'd be cut off from all that, as if it didn't exist. That always made me—right before a retreat—value it all the more.

A long walk was in order, a day of just hanging out. I needed to cool off anyway.

On the one hand, at that point in my life, I felt entirely at peace with sex. Years of sitting and staring at it had given me understanding, which would only deepen as I got older. On the other hand, I hadn't been with anyone for years, not on a long-term basis. I had the occasional summertime romance in Bar Harbor. But it was definitely not easy to find someone long-term up there. Jake had lucked out.

In the near future, of course, I might be living in Cambridge.

At one time—it was hard even to remember—sex had been an overwhelming compulsion and constant preoccupation in my life. I felt a need for it and was powerless to resist. Sometimes I would lie on my bed—as if to keep from walking out—and get the shakes, trying to resist. Mostly in those days I paid for it, but I also started a few affairs, thinking that if I could just set up the right situation, my ardor would cool off. That never happened. I'm sure it never would have.

What happens in meditation is that you watch and watch and watch, you watch some more, and finally, over months and years, things begin to break down. You begin with the situation Jess was in—overwhelmed by how chock-full of thinking your mind is—and what happens is not (as you hope) that the thought disappears, but that the mind gradually grows until thought isn't such a large part of it. It's still there, but off in the distance, quiet and subdued. Sometimes under difficult circumstances it gets noisy, but you know it's going to quiet down.

In the case of sex, at least my case, which may have been the only one of its kind ever (though I don't think so), it was overwhelmingly composed of thought. Thinking about sex was the way I'd escaped pain since I was a child. It had become so habitual, my mind did it automatically. In the difficulty of retreats my mind would seek out its old friend, and there I was, seeing those images for the millionth time.

I had thought of it as a physical compulsion—especially those days when I got the shakes—but often, as I sat through long days of meditation, I would be thinking *I need sex* and would look in my body for where the need was. (That was always Jake's suggestion. "See if you can locate it in the body.") Over my years of sitting the body had become a vast place of fascinating sensations. But I couldn't find the need for sex anywhere.

The male body does periodically need to ejaculate. There's a characteristic feeling of tension and pressure when it needs to, and apparently, if you don't take care of it, it will do so on its own. I've never understood the reason not to take care of it by yourself at least. It's so much fun!

But I found that my *need* for sex rarely had anything to do with the need to ejaculate. It wasn't a physical feeling at all.

I did find, through sitting, a whole universe of physical sensations at least as interesting as sexual ones. The energy that rushes through our body as we approach orgasm is present all the time, pleasurable quite apart from sex. By the time you discover the depth of various physical sensations, which are happening all the time, the images and thoughts of sex pale in comparison. They are present out of habit, but something much more interesting is going on.

I always had the feeling that various emotional events, including my father's death when I was sixteen, had numbed my body and cut me off from feeling. The only thing that could penetrate the numbness was sex, and it became my access to feeling. Now that I had discovered the world of feeling in my body, I still thought sex was wonderful, but hardly the only thing going on.

I covered a huge stretch of ground that day, not doing much of anything. I walked to Harvard Square and up to Davis. I walked on little streets up there, sat on benches and watched people go by, looked at squirrels and birds. The day was cold and cloudy, but I had a warm jacket and found the weather bracing. I stopped on my way back through Harvard Square for a light vegetarian wrap. I watched the chess master for a long time, watched other chess games. I was in front of the Y in plenty of time to meet Jake when he and Madeleine showed up.

He took a nap; I took a swim. We were meeting Josh at five thirty.

By the time we got to Green Street Josh was the life of the party, sitting at one of the stools we usually occupied and listening to everyone's opinions on scores of movies he had reviewed. (He spent his life doing this, he once told me.) Jess had identified him instantly; his picture ran with his column.

"Padre," Jess said when we walked in, and the whole crowd turned and bowed. It was their best performance yet. Josh, in the middle of the group, sat in khaki slacks and a green tweed sport jacket, laughing.

Jess hugged and kissed Jake. She hugged and kissed me, slapped my cheek a little when she did it. Our spat from earlier seemed forgotten. I don't know whether she'd found a man to take care of her, but she'd found the man she wanted now. She was flushed and beaming.

"How come you don't kiss us when we come in?" somebody asked.

"You're not this cute," Jess said, patting Jake's head. "And you don't have this cute a son."

"I got a cute son," the guy said.

"He looks like he got whacked with a tire iron," somebody said.

"By the same guy whacked you, only harder."

"Where'd you get that kid, anyway?" somebody said to me. "Where'd he get that red hair?"

"Red-haired milkman," another guy said.

"Father Jake, you got any sons?"

"He's a priest, for Christ's sake."

"That should stop him?"

"No sons that I know of," Jake said. Jess had brought his Guinness, and he sipped it.

"Maybe a daughter or two," somebody said.

"The modern era of movies," Josh said. "Is it a great one? That was the topic before you guys came in and knocked us into the gutter."

The discussion went around about that for a while. There was the usual argument—which I actually agreed with—that the golden age of American cinema was the late sixties and early seventies, when a number of us had been young. Movies had more depth then. Now they were derived from TV and comic books.

Josh argued—rather persuasively—that we were forgetting a lot of mindless crap. He admitted the new filmmakers based their work on popular culture—filmmakers always had—but they knew the form and used the technology better than older filmmakers had. He thought that when all was said and done, there would be as many great films from his generation as from ours. They wouldn't all be American, but they'd be plentiful.

It was startling how knowledgeable and astute that crowd of barflies was. It was not surprising how argumentative they were. It took us forty-five minutes to get out of there and into the restaurant proper. I noticed as we were leaving that Josh gave his card to Jess. He turned away, and she winked at me.

Another reason I was glad I hadn't fucked her that morning.

Jake had also noticed. "She's the girl for you," he said when we got to the table.

"You don't think she's a little young?" Josh asked.

"Not from what I've heard. Compared to your usual."

"She does lack focus at the moment," I said. "Her life's in disarray."

"That's temporary," Jake said. "We're working on it."

Jake had asked her in the midst of our movie discussion if she was looking forward to the next day.

"I'm totally fucking petrified," she said. "Pardon my French."

"Just show up," Jake said. "That's the only important thing. We'll take care of you."

Exactly what I'd said. When Jake said it, she listened.

Josh's feelings about Jake were complicated. On the one hand, way back when he used to come and visit in Bar Harbor, he called him Uncle Jake, used him as a confidant and mentor far more than even I knew. On the other hand, he thought I'd gone way overboard and that Jake had led me into it. When he was in college, in particular, he'd had an anti-Jake phase, as his father got weirder and weirder.

Now he seemed reconciled to the man. His father was weird and he wasn't fighting it anymore. Maybe, if this new center became a reality, I'd be downright respectable.

One thing I admired about Jake—and hoped to emulate—was that he never pushed practice on anyone. He was as helpful as possible if the other person brought it up. But if it didn't come up he never so much as mentioned it.

The wish to practice has to come from inside, he always said. Otherwise it won't take.

"What's this your father tells me about your being burnt out?" Jake asked. I'd filled him in on our earlier conversation. "You didn't sound burnt out at the bar."

"I don't know that it's burnt out. That might be Dad's term. But there's something weird. Something wrong."

He went on to describe his malaise. The whole thing with Mitzi was a repeat of previous performances. He was doing his work, still loved movies, but felt a sense of repetition in that too. The inevitable crap bothered him more than ever, and he dismissed it too harshly. Even when he liked movies, he praised them with the same words he'd used before.

"There are only so many ways you can say something's good," he said. "That's a reviewer's nightmare."

"Is somebody keeping track?"

"I am."

"People don't remember what they read in the paper. Just the feeling from it."

"I know. I worry about it too much."

In the midst of that conversation we ordered and got our food, blazing hot—the chef was known for his spices—an absolutely delicious pork tenderloin for me, with yams and beans and apples. We had a second beer. It was an odd prelude to a retreat.

"I think you ought to write a novel," Jake said.

"A *novel?* Who reads them?"

"A screenplay. Something. Write a book about the movies. What you were saying out there."

"I've said all that in columns."

"A book is different. It'll reach a different audience."

Again, that was one of those things that, if I had said it, would have sounded like a father's hectoring. From Jake it had a different tone. But you could tell, by the way Josh paused, and the energy that came into his posture—even by the way he resisted—that he'd thought of this himself. Jake was telling him to do what he already knew to do. He needed someone to tell him.

"When would I do it?"

"You've got to have time in your day. Movies don't show all the time."

"It might take energy from my other work."

"Your other work isn't using you up."

"My reviews might suffer."

"I think they'd be better. Enriched by what you were doing."

"My life would get more complicated."

"Only for a while. And you'd have control of that. There wouldn't be any hurry."

"What if it didn't work out?"

"Then it didn't. Who would know? You've still got the other job."

Everything Josh came up with Jake had an answer for; there was a certain rightness to what the man was saying, and Josh knew it.

Josh was definitely energized. His whole affect was different.

"Or maybe I'm full of shit," Jake said. "Who knows? It's just an idea."

The final statement that drove the argument home.

Dessert at that place was as good as the dinner. Jake had some kind of chocolate concoction—I didn't catch the name—that may finally have satisfied his craving. I had one bite, and it satisfied mine.

The bar as we walked out was as jammed as the night before. Jess could only blow us a kiss as we left. She gave Josh a big smile.

"I want you to think over what we talked about in there," Jake said out on the sidewalk.

"I will," Josh said.

"There's a moment in your life when you've got to jump into the dark. Otherwise things go stale."

"Yeah."

"Stay open to the situation and you'll find it."

Jake gave Josh a hug. He barely came up to his chest.

"Don't go too nuts looking at that wall," Josh said.

"You're late with that," Jake said. "I'm way over the deep end."

"Then keep an eye on my old man. He's the one I'm worried about."

"He's about to go."

There was a statement to ponder.

14

OF ALL THE THINGS I dislike about the work I do—if it is work, which I often doubt—wearing robes is right up there. I don't wear them often, just on occasions when we have a retreat or a teaching weekend. I always feel as if I'm playing dress-up, like when I strapped on my six shooters and ten-gallon hat as a kid. I feel like a fraud. It's my problem, of course. I'm just playing a role, in a particular situation.

I'd better get used to it.

The thing about Jake was that he never seemed to be wearing robes. He had them on, undeniably, and there are all kinds of adjustments you have to make about sitting, walking, bowing, everything we do. But he seemed entirely comfortable. He wore even the most elaborate robes in a relaxed way. They looked as natural on him as the jeans and sweatshirt he wore around the bike shop.

We had some senior students taking care of logistics, like *sesshin* opening instructions, so all we had to do was show up. We had picked up our stuff from the Y and walked up to Madeleine's, me carrying the suitcases and Jake the sacks that held our cushions, went straight to the bedrooms and changed. Jake had a glint in his eye when I stopped by his room, a big smile on his face. He took delight in the weirdest things. You'd have thought we were headed for the movies, or a ballgame.

We stopped in a small room beside the meditation hall, lit some incense at an altar and made our way in, Jake offering the incense at the large altar in the hall. There was only the dimmest background lighting, the altar candle flickering against the wall. Jake did three floor bows, and we took our places.

The zendo—this long, wide room that had once been a living room—was beautifully arranged. There were cushions around the outside walls; down the middle were adjustable room dividers that gave us more wall space, though we needed it only for some part-time people, like Jess. The tradition in Soto Zen, ever since Bodhidharma supposedly stared at the side of a cave for nine years, is that we gaze at a wall, differentiating us from all other forms of Buddhism (*there's* an important distinction for you). But on that first night it was our custom to face the center, holding our heads up but gazing toward the floor. It was the first sitting in what would be seven days of sitting and walking.

And it was the only sitting during which Jake spoke. Fifteen minutes in, he cleared his throat.

"When I say good-bye to someone before *sesshin*," he said, "I say it as if it may be the last time." I thought of the way he had hugged Josh outside the restaurant, slapping his back, looking into his eyes. "As if I'm sitting on my deathbed, that person walking out the door. *Sesshin* is like death, it's the best preparation for death. Also the best preparation for life.

"For seven days we'll be apart from our normal life. Whatever is going on out there, whatever is bothering you, troubling you, exciting you, there's nothing you can do about it. We'll drop everything as if it doesn't exist, see what it's like just to be here as a sitting, breathing body."

He didn't say anything for a few minutes—I thought he was through—then spoke again.

"Years ago, I was in a little town in Mexico. I had just gotten back from Japan, was bumming around for a while, went down there from California. In the middle of the town, every morning, an Indian woman came to beg in front of the church. She was tiny, not much over four feet, and seemed old, in her sixties or seventies. She would sit in front of the church and hold her right hand in a begging position, like a mudra, staring in front of herself. I stood and watched her for minutes at a time. Her back was straight. Her posture was strong. I never saw her move.

"If you gave her money, she looked up and beamed, radiantly. She was full of life. But she never asked for money. She never asked for anything. She just sat, while life went on all around. Somehow, sitting there, she took part in the fullness of life.

"I had been in Japan for years and knew people who were quite impressed with their ability to sit, but had never seen anyone sit better than that woman did every day. She wasn't a Buddhist. She had no training. Just a human being, who in all her years had learned something about life. So in the spirit of that woman, with no idea if anything is going to show up in our hands, let's sit for the next few days. Let's ask nothing of life, and see what it offers us."

I had never heard that story before. In all the years I'd known him, he'd never used it. I couldn't imagine why. It was perfect.

For another twenty minutes we sat in the flickering candlelight, then the timekeeper rang the bell, we did some bowing and chanted the Refuges, then Jake and I went up to our rooms. About half of the group would be heading home. Others would scatter around the building in sleeping bags. We'd start again at six.

The rooms where we were staying were quite large, included dressers, writing desks, queen-sized beds. Each had its own bathroom. It made you wonder why we'd been staying at the Y, though Jake said from the start he wanted to keep some distance from Madeleine. But after the narrow metal bed frames, sagging mattresses, communal showers, smells of disinfectant, this seemed like paradise.

I often don't sleep well on the first night of *sesshin*, but I conked out immediately that night, didn't wake up until somebody came around with the wake-up bell at five fifteen.

I love the energy of the early morning. The hard time on retreat—if I'm going to have one—is late afternoon, when I've been in that little room for hours and will be there for hours more. But the early morning, with sunlight streaming in the windows and birds singing their morning songs, my body slowly growing used to waking life, seems the perfect part of the day for *zazen*. I could sit forever.

That day, of course, I had the dharma talk looming at ten thirty. It sat like an abyss waiting to swallow me. But there was literally no way I could prepare except by sitting, so that's what I did.

After two morning sittings—with ten minutes of walking in between—we had our long service of bowing and chanting, about twenty minutes, followed by breakfast, which was served *oryoki* style, as we sat at our places. Darcy had flavored the oatmeal with what seemed to be almond butter and maple syrup, and Jake took a second bowl, which I'd almost never seen him do. The fruit bowl was also elaborate: apples, pears, bananas, grapes, peaches and blueberries from the end of the summer, a few strawberries, everything smothered in yogurt. It was delicious, close to a no no for Zen. But Jake ate it up—so to speak—taking seconds on the fruit too. Maybe Darcy *was* the true Zen cook.

Jess showed up at nine, right after the breakfast break, an hour before I'd expected. I was the officiating priest that day—Jake and I were alternating—facing into the room while everyone else faced the wall. Jess looked both nervous and determined, didn't seem to have slept a lot. The room was full—weekends in general were more crowded, as were the mornings—and she seemed fine, though you never know what's going on in someone's head.

The other person I had my eye on was a young guy named Kevin. He'd sat with us before, and that day had served breakfast. There was something in his slouching body language, trying to be casual, also in his lazy eyes, that seemed terribly sad. You pick up on things on retreat. Some people have sat a lot and are hard to read, doing their best imitation of a Zen master, but others are transparent, their hearts not on their sleeves but on their whole bodies. Kevin drew your sympathy just by the way he looked.

At ten thirty it was time for the talk. Some teachers go off to prepare during the sitting before the talk, have a look at some notes, even sit off somewhere and practice it, but Jake just stayed in his place. He didn't use notes, actually believed that, however much he pondered or went over things beforehand, he should sit down to deliver the talk with nothing, let it come out of nowhere.

We have a ceremony before the talk begins. The students gathered their cushions in a semicircle around the teacher's place, and we entered in the same procession as before, me holding incense, Jake following and offering it at the altar, doing three bows. Normally I would sit in the crowd, but today I sat beside him; Jake said something about that right after the short chant that begins the talks.

"Hank is going to help with the talks this week."

Hank at that point probably couldn't have spoken at all. My heart was thumping like a bass drum, my palms wet, the soles of my feet actually wet—a new one on me—and that nervous feeling fluttered down in my stomach.

But I have come to feel through the years that fear is what connects me with the audience, also somehow with what I'm talking about. The words come from where the fear is. So I don't worry about it. If I'd had to speak right then, I'd have waited. Your heart can't pound forever.

Jess sat straight and looked relaxed, now that there was some entertainment. Kevin seemed on the verge of sleep. Madeleine—out in the middle of the crowd—looked intent. Thirty or so faces around them were in various stages of concentration, expectation, intensity.

"Today is the first day of *sesshin*," Jake said, "and by this time you're already disappointed." A burst of laughter from the group. They were ready for one. "We come looking for something, wisdom, compassion, peace of mind, calm. Maybe you had something you wanted to work on. There's something going on that you want to figure out, or get away from.

"But whatever that is, whatever you were hoping for, chances are it hasn't happened. What you want to happen is not what happens. The wanting itself is an obstacle. It's the wanting you need to look at. *It's* the problem, not the thing you want to fix."

There was a long pause. I wondered if Jake had spaced out. I wasn't sure how I was going to decide.

I looked out at Madeleine, who still looked calm. When she worried, I would.

"What you should do over the next few days," Jake said, "is as little as possible. Expend the least amount of effort you can. Just stay on the cushion. I know that sounds strange, but most people who come to Zen try too hard, and the teaching is that we're enlightened as we are. There's nothing to do. We just settle into ourselves."

Another long pause. When Jake spoke, he held the little wooden stick that teachers carry in front of him, as if planting it in the ground. He held it with two hands, like a little post.

"One of the most interesting things about the Buddha's teaching is that it starts with the realization of impermanence. He set out from his home, set out from the palace, because he had some deep experience of impermanence. It had shaken him to the core.

"It was something so deep that, even though he had everything, a beautiful wife, a newborn son, position at the top of his society, wealth, luxury, every advantage, he left all that to shave his head, walk around in discarded clothing, and beg for a living. He gave up everything because of the question he had encountered: If old age, sickness, and death are the fate of mankind, what's the use of living?"

Jake gazed at the wall in the back of the room. He took a long pause.

"It's a young man's question, in a way. An old man doesn't ask it. But he didn't come up with an answer for impermanence. He didn't, as he thought he might, go into meditation so deeply he found something. He actually found impermanence to be at the heart of everything. He made it the cornerstone of his teaching."

Another long pause, another gaze at the back wall.

"That's what Hank is going to talk about this morning."

I looked at him. He was holding that little stake in front of him, staring down. He wasn't, as far as I could tell, having one of his spells. He looked as calm and clear-eyed as he had all morning. He actually smiled at me, that little glint in his eye.

What the hell was this?

I had been caught up in what he was saying, especially the part about it being a young man's question. I wondered where he would go with that. I wanted to hear.

If I was going to, it would have to come out of me.

I didn't feel nervous. I had done that already, felt fear down to the seventh sphincter or whatever it was. I still felt a twinge of that sensation, a little hollow feeling, down beneath my balls, down there, as we used to say, where I live. I had no idea what to say.

I took a deep breath and spoke.

"The most interesting thing about the teaching on impermanence is the way the Buddha taught us to see it. Or maybe just the most effective thing, I don't know. Lots of thinkers have talked about impermanence. Poets have been writing about it for centuries. And Heraclitus, who I first studied in college, is famous for saying you can't step twice in the same river. I remember how fascinated I was when I first came across that statement. Pondered it for hours. It was my first encounter with the emptiness behind everything. Reading about it in a book, anyway."

Well, maybe not hours. I had a tendency toward hyperbole. I also wasn't certain when Heraclitus lived, whether he preceded the Buddha. Maybe that wasn't the point.

The room was deadly still, everyone in their best Zen postures. A few looked at me, but most were gazing at the floor, terribly serious. It was like lecturing a crowd of zombies.

"The Buddha taught us to see impermanence not just in a flowing river, or the ruins of a town, or the fleeting nature of love, where poets often find it, but in our own experience. The moment-by-moment life of this fathom-long body. You don't have to wait for a civilization to crumble. You can just watch your body and mind for a while.

"You sit down hoping to find enlightenment, and a few seconds later you're wondering what's for lunch. You catch a glimpse of the void, then your knee starts to hurt, you get caught up in that. You spend a few moments following the breath and you hear the basketball game outside; suddenly you're in a game you played thirty years ago, with the guys you went to the playground with, from around the old neighborhood. A simple noise from outside and you're in another world. It's uncanny."

There was a feeling of immense space in the room. I spoke a sentence and it floated off toward the ceiling. There was a pause, and I'd speak another. I was actually talking at a normal pace, but everything seemed to have slowed down. There were spaces between words, abysses between sentences.

Maybe I was catatonic.

"Which of those people is you? The one who wants enlightenment or the one who would settle for a bowl of soup? The one who's a good meditator, or the one who would give up anything, the whole *sesshin*, practice itself, if only his knee stops hurting? The one who feels compassion for every soul on earth or the one who would like to kill the person sitting next to you, he's moving so much? Which is it?"

I was starting to roll. I could feel the energy.

"It's interesting the way one Buddhist teaching leads to another, you're talking about impermanence and suddenly you're into no-self, you switch to the fact of suffering and you're back at impermanence. The teachings lock together, so that you agree in the beginning to a simple proposition, you can't find anything in your body and mind that's permanent, and that snowballs into the fact that you don't have a self. There's something brilliant about it."

I'd been deeply moved by the teachings of the Buddha when I finally found them, near the age of forty. No other religion had held together for me, as much as I tried to find one. Suddenly there was this teaching that seemed simple and profound, also airtight.

"I remember how terrified I was when I finally saw the concept of no-self. At the same time, it was a huge relief. Whatever I'd thought about myself, whoever I'd thought I was, I could just let go. Even the fear I was feeling at that very moment. Fear is a reaction that arises. I'm afraid of heights; maybe you're afraid of deep water, or dark streets. It's not who you are, it arises under conditions. It's a fact of being human. There's no such thing as a fearful person."

I stopped for a moment, thought about it.

"So who are you, if you're none of that? You're none of the things you've been thinking you are all these years?"

The immensity of that question filled the room, at least for me. It also left me with nothing to say, but a lot more time left, so I doubled back to the Buddha's life, where the subject started. I began to speak more conventionally.

What I think is that the legendary story of the Buddha's encounter with impermanence—that his father kept him from sickness, aging, and death until he was in his late twenties, when the gods intervened—was a fairy tale that pointed to a deeper truth. He had seen those things, as everyone does, but they hadn't touched him, cushioned as he was by a life of luxury. Finally, in his late twenties, some incident deeply touched him.

We don't think of ourselves as princes, but his life didn't compare to the luxury we have today. Our comforts seem to protect us, but really they dull blows we need to feel. Cultures where life is more primal, death more random, have a deeper understanding. We're more like the young Buddha.

But when he did see death, it hit him all the harder.

All spiritual life begins with that shock of impermanence. We see that our loved ones will die, we will die: nothing in our world lasts forever. What was striking about the Buddha—the most remarkable thing about his life—was that he couldn't leave that fact alone. He had to face the question of impermanence and left his palace to do it, left a beautiful wife, a newborn son.

His subsequent experience, though it seems foreign and strange, was actually typical: his early study of meditation, working to achieve deep states, was like what lots of meditators do; his ascetic period, when he blotted out desire with intense effort, reflects another strategy they adopt. We don't go to the lengths he did, but experience those stages. The Buddha's life is archetypal and exemplary.

Finally he discovered that simple, clear awareness—something he'd had all along, but had neglected—was the key to practice. It didn't answer the question of impermanence (it wasn't a question), but he saw the fact of it, in every aspect of life. It was that clear seeing, resisting nothing, that opened him to the abundance of life.

I wandered around in different aspects of this story. By the time I got to his teaching—the moment he saw that truth and went back into the world—my time was up. It was time to expound on impermanence and my talk was over.

Whatever you do in *sesshin*, you have lots of time to think about it. The talk was followed by a thirty-minute sitting, then of course we did lunch in silence, so I spent that whole time wondering what I'd said, trying to remember what it was, wondering if I'd phrased things correctly, imagining how I could have done differently, wondering what Jake thought. None of which was any help whatsoever, but my mind kept doing it. I had to go through it.

After lunch there was a break, and Jake stepped for a moment into my room.

"I didn't even get to the teaching," I said. "I went back too far."

"You'll have another chance. What you said was good."

"They didn't hear the subject of your talk."

"They've heard me enough."

"I wish I could do it over."

"You can. You'll be doing it the rest of your life. It doesn't matter how you do."

That made a hell of a lot of sense—I was sitting there teaching our students; it didn't matter how I did?

He touched my chest. "Trust what you come up with," he said. "It's all you've got."

There was a work period after lunch break. I went out and raked leaves on the grounds, did some work in the garden. I've always thought a perfect meditation retreat would include an Olympic pool for lap swimming, but I guess you can't have everything. I did manage to do some simple yoga. The danger, on the first day especially, is that you'll tighten up. I tried to exercise as much as I could. I had taken a walk at morning break, would do so again in the evening.

I was doing *dokusan* that day, the short interview the teacher has with students. We did it in a small room off the front hallway, the same place Jake and I stopped for incense. The first three students who came in were old-timers, just wanted to check their postures, ask some simple questions. Mostly on the first day people were settling in.

The fourth person was Jess.

Of all her wardrobe changes, this one seemed the most extreme. She had on a white sweatshirt and blue sweatpants, absolutely no makeup. You could see the various little holes from her piercings. Her hair was combed out over her shoulders. Her eyes looked tired.

She was supposed to do a floor bow to the altar, various other gestures, but just plopped down on the cushion.

In an hour or two she'd be pumping beer at the Green Street Grill.

"Is this where you ask me some impossible question?" she asked. "How to clap one hand?"

"That's another kind of Zen," I said.

"So what do we do? I assume we still can't fuck."

"Jess," I said. "You never quit."

"If this doesn't make you want to, nothing ever will. You don't have any dope back here, do you? Some booze?"

"We're clean. It's just you and me."

"I can't do this. I'm sorry. I wanted to. I wanted to be like my mother. But I can't."

"Why should you be like your mother?"

"I was fired up when I came here. I actually came early. Did you see?"

"I did."

"But I swear to God, as God is my witness, if there even is a God in this stupid religion, I haven't followed a breath all day. Not one."

"At least you're consistent."

"I was nervous when I got here, I admit. Jittered up and knew it might take a while. All those bull dykes around. Do you have any idea how many lesbians there are in that room?"

Jake, for some reason, attracted women followers. He had started out with women and others followed, maybe because they were friends. I hadn't checked up on their sexual orientation.

"How many? I asked.

"A shitload. Not that I mind. Some of my best friends, I'm sure. It's just surprising. Like it's dyke night at the bar. I still thought I'd settle down after a while. I haven't."

"You've done this for a total of two or three hours."

"My mind is like a juke box. Every song I ever heard. I've also been over every relationship I've had with a guy, and believe me, there have been a few."

No doubt.

"My knees hurt. My back aches. My ass has a cramp the size of a softball. And I'm supposed to do this four more days? I don't think so."

"You're asking a lot of yourself."

"To follow one breath? Not to switch off to every blow job I've ever given?"

"To come here and meditate for a day. Even half a day. Most people start with ten minutes."

"I'm telling you I can't do ten minutes. I can't do one minute. I can't do one second. Are you getting this?"

"You're meeting yourself, Jess. You're seeing your mind. It's not a pretty sight. It never is."

"You think all those dykes are out there dreaming of pussy? Do I want to sit next to them?"

"I don't know what they're doing. I don't know what anyone's doing. But the experience you're having is normal."

"*Normal?*"

"You're right on track."

"Jesus."

"Come less tomorrow. Sleep in a little."

"I couldn't sleep. That's why I came."

"Leave early. Leave after the work period. You've got to take it easy."

"I had no idea what you were saying in that talk. I mean, it was nice. But all this is so new. Why don't you make jokes, like Padre?"

Another boost for my confidence. "I'll try to make some jokes."

"You've got to start at the beginning. All this stuff about the Buddha. I don't know what it is."

I thought I had started at the beginning. I thought that was the problem.

"Forget it," she said. "The problem is me. I'm fucked up."

"You're not fucked up. Just a human being."

"It's the same thing. Anyway. I don't think you'll be seeing me tomorrow."

"That would be fine."

"I'm more like a bar girl. That's where you can find me."

"That's where I'll look."

"And we *should* have fucked, by the way. You don't know what you missed."

This had to be one of the more unusual *dokusans* in the history of Buddhism.

Jess was getting up, slowly. She did seem a tad sore.

"By the way, some dyke tried to tell me what to do when I came in here, but I didn't listen. My brain was on tilt. I apologize."

165

"It's okay."

"Say good-bye to Padre. Tell him I love him."

"I will."

"I love you too. But fuck you in your skinny little ass for ever suggesting I do this."

"I didn't suggest it."

"You guys should be shot for promoting this."

She opened the door and stepped out, limping.

What a gal. Jake was right. Most people come in and pretend to be spiritual. That honesty would take her a long way.

I had been hoping Kevin might come, but he didn't. I always seemed, in any *sesshin*, to find a young man to look after. Maybe looking for a second son.

The last person to come in, at eight fifteen, was Madeleine.

She was the opposite of Jess. Her face immaculately made up, every hair in place. She looked exactly as she had that morning. She wore a white cotton outfit—blouse and slacks—with a flower pattern on the blouse. She bowed to the altar, sat gingerly in front of me.

"This is the first time we've done this," she said.

"It is."

"Usually I talk to Jake."

To say the least. She never sat a whole *sesshin*, but talked to him two or three times a day.

"Nothing against you," she said.

"I know."

"You're qualified. Jake told me."

I shrugged. "I'm not so sure."

"You think I could see him?"

"You could ask. He wanted me to take the first day. I could ask for you."

"It's all right. I'll be fine."

There was a long pause. She sat there, looking down.

"This is the first time I've sat a whole day," she said.

"That's wonderful."

"You must think I'm silly."

"I don't."

"Must wonder what's wrong with me."

"I don't, Madeleine."

"I'm just so, I don't know, afraid. I'm so frightened, of this one thing. But I don't know what it is."

I nodded. It was everything.

"Even now, I don't know if I can go back in that room."

"I'm frightened too."

"Not like this, Henry."

"My palms were sweating when I gave that talk. My *feet* were sweating. If I'd stood up I would have slid to the floor."

She laughed. "We're a mess. We're both a mess. What are we going to do without him?"

"I don't know." I shook my head.

We sat a while longer.

"Do you have any advice?" she asked.

"Nothing you haven't heard before. Be with your fear. Let it be. Feel it in your body."

She gave a little bow. "That does sound familiar."

"It should."

"I thought your talk was good. I was surprised."

I smiled.

"I didn't mean it that way."

She did mean it that way. She just didn't mean to say it.

"I was surprised you *gave* the talk. I thought Jake was fine. He didn't miss a beat."

I'd felt the same way.

"I wonder what will happen tomorrow."

She wasn't the only one.

15

THAT WAS THE WAY the days went, chanting before all the meals and at the end of the day, a talk at midmorning and work period in the afternoon, otherwise just sitting and walking. When you first do it, as Jess could have told you, it can be one of the most hair-raising things you've ever done, sitting there staring at your mind by the hour, but once you've done it a few times, you see that it doesn't have much to do with you, it's a ritual celebration of ordinary life.

Sitting, standing, walking, lying down. Eating, working, listening. Everything is reduced to its most basic components, so you finally notice them. One of the things I first noticed is how profoundly in touch with the rhythm of the day *sesshin* is. The whole of life is that way in monasteries. It lets you know the day has a rhythm, that you live better when you're in synch with it.

At the beginning of the morning, before we headed down, Jake said, "I think you should do *dokusan* again today."

"People will be disappointed," I said.

"They can deal with it."

"Madeleine would like to see you."

"She can see me. I'm not saying I won't see people. But she sat all day yesterday. She's never done that before."

I nodded.

"She might use me to get her off the hook," he said.

The thought had occurred to me.

Kevin signed up for *dokusan* first thing, and normally I would have waited until the afternoon, but I'd noticed him so much that I decided to go ahead before the dharma talk.

He was a tall, good-looking guy, wore four or five days' growth of beard, though I think that was intentional, the way young guys like that rough look. He was thin and seemed relaxed, but looked terminally sleepy, his head lolling as if he would keel over any minute. He had the same lackadaisical look when he served meals, as if trying to be casual. I had the feeling he wasn't quite entering into things.

He did all of the bows in the *dokusan* room, but when he sat before me started lolling. He almost put me to sleep.

"How's it going?" I asked.

"Not bad. I've been a little sleepy."

No kidding.

"This isn't your first *sesshin*," I said.

"My sixth. The third with you guys. The problem is . . ." He smiled a little. "The first one was, like, bliss."

"Really?"

"I keep wanting that again. I know it's a mistake."

"Hard not to."

Talk about problems you don't often run into.

"I love this group. Just being around them. It's like a family. A loving family."

This bunch of bull dykes?

"How's your own family?" I asked.

"I don't really have one. My mom died when I was little. Dad tried to be what I needed but wasn't up to it. He's a businessman. Nice guy."

"He never married again?"

"Never."

What an upbringing.

"I thought of that when you talked yesterday," he said, "about the Buddha's experience of impermanence. How he went through it. Followed the question to the end. I didn't do that. Didn't get too far."

"How old were you?"

"Seven."

I shook my head. So sad.

"Any brothers or sisters?"

"I'm the only one."

It got worse and worse. Living all those years with a father who himself didn't get past what happened. It was no wonder he liked sitting with a group of women. Even if they were all silent and got together only a couple of times per year.

What he looked like was a six-foot-two-inch child.

He needed a man's love. He needed Jake.

"Does it come up when you sit? About your mother?"

"I have the feeling I'd go nuts if it did. Really berserk."

"That would be bad?"

"I don't know. Going nuts in the zendo? Doesn't sound like the best."

He smiled, sleepily. "I have the idea," he said, "maybe it's all wrong, that practice is away from that. Away from personal problems, moving toward something larger."

"You get to the larger thing through the problems."

"I don't know. That's the only way?"

"There are ways of going berserk that don't disrupt the zendo."

Jess could tell him about that. Maybe a good dose of Jess was what Kevin needed.

She'd probably blow him away. She'd definitely blow him.

"So your advice is what?" He smiled again. "I should go nuts?"

"Don't do anything. Just let things come up as they do. You can't really stop them." No matter how sleepy you get.

"I guess."

"Don't try to have a blissful experience. That was an accident."

It happened because he was holding things off. He couldn't do that forever.

He bowed to me, looking more puzzled than when he came in.

Things seemed to be proceeding as they should. He seemed a long way from going nuts.

Once again before the dharma talk, Jake offered the incense and did the floor bows. I'm not sure why, if he was just going to turn things over.

"Yesterday we spoke about impermanence," he said. "The first of the Four Noble Truths. One of the three marks of existence. Those are more a part of Theravada teaching than Zen, though they're basic to any understanding of Buddhism.

"The Buddha was a great list maker, at a time when all teaching was oral. He numbered everything so people could remember. Zen tends to do away with lists. And I think that if you understand impermanence, everything follows from that. You don't need the other parts. Look at impermanence well, or look at suffering, the things he went off to examine when he left the palace."

Jake sat holding that stick in front of him, as if getting ready to shift into high. He seemed utterly relaxed.

"In Zen we say the answer to death is to die now," he said. "That's our answer to the problem of impermanence. Anyway, that's what Hank will talk about today. The question of impermanence, how the Buddha confronts it, what it means to die now."

I was starting to think the whole thing was a put-on. All the stuff about Jake's spells, his problems with his memory. He had made that up so he could get me to give these talks, on subjects he picked. For two days I hadn't seen a shred of evidence he was having trouble. He hadn't missed a bow or stumbled over a word. He seemed fine.

I sat there knowing he was going to toss the ball to me, feeling the anxiety crawl around in my stomach. I felt fine until he said the thing about dying now. That was one of those Zen slogans everybody said but no one understood. If I didn't deal with it, I'd be doing the same thing as the day before. Pulling back before I attacked the question.

"Dying now means coming to each moment fresh," I said. "Seeing every person, even your partner, as if you've never met before. Hearing the birds as if you've never heard a chirp in your life. Our past is what we think of as our life, that whole life of thought and memory that we carry around all the time, but nothing actually repeats itself. Every moment is new, and you can't live this moment until you die to the past one."

"That's not what you said in *dokusan*. That's the whole thing I've been trying to do. Except that, shit, I wasn't supposed to talk now. I'm sorry." Kevin sat red-faced, a few feet in front of me.

At least he hadn't fallen asleep.

"Normally we let the teachers give the talk before we pin them to the wall," Jake said.

"I know. I know that. I spaced out," Kevin said.

"We didn't have question-and-answer yesterday," a woman in the back said. "That might be part of the confusion."

"Time was up," Jake said. "Hank ended where he thought he should. Maybe we'll have time for questions today."

I didn't think any of this would be happening if Jake had been giving the talk.

I also thought I had to answer Kevin, however much that would take the talk in a different direction. "Sometimes what you meet in this moment is something from the past," I said. "That especially happens on retreat. The whole thing is a setup, primed to bring up what you want to avoid, to bring up your suffering. It's also a chance to encounter and transform it.

"When something from the past comes up, especially some difficult thing, it's often because you haven't assimilated it. The feeling around it. We tend to do that as human beings, not let feelings in. We block them with our bodies, by tightening. So what you do as you sit is let everything in. Soften to the whole experience. Then you won't tighten."

As I said that, I noticed Jess sitting back in the crowd, two tears rolling down her cheeks. Her eyes looked even more tired and vulnerable than the day before.

She could have told Kevin what he needed. She did it naturally.

Again I waded into a familiar subject, again I faced a roomful of zombies doing *zazen*, but the experience was entirely different. I didn't feel the vast space in the room, though it was still there. It was as if the room had shrunk way down, to the size of the *dokusan* room, and I was sitting there with just Kevin and Jess, one who needed to surrender to the process, one who needed to pull herself together.

Those were the two characteristic responses to *sesshin*, fighting it or collapsing altogether. Almost everyone does one or the other, and practice is learning how to fine-tune that. But it was as if I were speaking to the two of them in a conversational voice. No one else was there. They had all disappeared.

I hadn't known what I would say when I began. Somehow, just by staying with that place of fear, that deep place in the pit of my stomach where all the anxiety crawled around, I came up with a talk.

Jess wiped away her tears at the beginning. She still seemed deeply tired, moved around a lot. But she listened to every word, as did Kevin. They were my audience.

Madeleine, I'd have to say, was not. She was the person I'd have tried not to look at if Jake hadn't long ago told me to make eye contact all over the room. She was one person I thought was holding it up against the talk Jake would have given, seeing his as better (I did too). I knew she needed what I said as much as anyone. But I felt her as a judge, criticizing everything. That was the voice I didn't want to hear.

After all the fuss about a question-and-answer session, there wasn't time anyway, and there were no questions. People were ready for lunch, was the feeling I had.

The first person who came in for *dokusan* after work period—wouldn't you know—was Madeleine, the cat who jumps into the lap of the one person who doesn't like cats.

Again her outfit was elegant, her demeanor impeccable, her bow to the altar perfect. She had superb posture as she sat in front of me.

"I thought Jake would give *dokusan* today," she said.

"I did too. He told me this morning I should."

"He's getting you ready."

That did seem to be the plan.

"I don't know if I can do this," she said. "Honestly. I'm ready to jump out of my skin."

Of all the people in the room, she was the last one I would have picked to say such a thing. The second day can be difficult, muscles sore, fatigue starting to set in. The end looks a long way away. Some people in the room looked jittery, some on the verge of collapse. Madeleine looked the soul of composure.

She couldn't let down. That was her problem.

"This is unfair to you, I know," she said. "But I was so hoping Jake would be in this room."

I could have gotten him. I could have told her they could meet later. Somehow that didn't seem what she needed.

"Try to describe what you're going through," I said.

"It's going to sound crazy."

"Believe me, Madeleine. It can't be crazier than things I've seen in myself."

"It's this feeling of utter panic, like the walls are closing in. The room seems small. My place looks small. The people around me too close. The wall is right in front of me."

"Yes."

"It was all I could do yesterday afternoon not to run from

the room and scream. Throw myself out the window. The weird thing is that this is my house. I've lived here for years. It never felt this way."

She had spent her whole life getting away from it. Going off to do business, visiting exotic places. She'd never really sat in it.

"The only way I got through yesterday was thinking I'd see Jake today. Now I'm wondering if I'll see him tomorrow. If I'll see him at all. I had this retreat specifically to talk to him; I've spent the last eight weeks planning for it, and now I can't see him."

She'd spent the last three days talking to him. How much did she want?

"I wanted this to be the retreat I really sat, now that Jake had agreed to come and teach. But I don't know if I can do that without him. Don't know if I can stand it."

She was like me in that cabin on Mount Desert, the summer I met Jake. I might as well have been staying in a shoebox.

The thing that's small is your mind. That's where you're enclosing yourself.

"Sometimes Jake teaches with his presence," I said. "Sometimes his absence."

"I prefer presence."

Apparently.

"But I've got to tell you, Madeleine. The fear you're describing, exactly what you've told me about, is the whole thing Zen is set up to make you feel."

"That can't be."

"That's why it's so claustrophobic. It leaves you at your place the whole time. In the old zendos they used to sleep there. Some places you couldn't lie down."

"I'd have gone stark raving mad."

"There's a whole world out there waiting for you to step into it, to step through the walls that are holding you back.

They seem to be reinforced concrete. They're actually tissue paper. Totally imaginary."

She stared at me. Didn't seem to be buying.

"The only way to get out there is to go through this fear. Completely experience it, until you're done."

"I know what you're saying is true."

"You'll already be in that larger world. But you've got to feel this now. Keep coming back until you feel it. Until it's commonplace, like any other feeling."

She groaned.

"This isn't your fear," I said. "It isn't mine, although I've felt it. It's human fear. Part of being in the world."

I didn't seem to have registered at all.

"I appreciate this, Henry. You've been helpful."

"You're actually quite brave, Madeleine. The bravest person in that room."

"You're trying to encourage me."

"I mean it. Bravery isn't when you don't feel fear. It's when you face it."

She bowed, tried to smile, stepped out.

I meant what I'd said. She could only hear it from Jake.

Late in the afternoon, Jess came in. She was wearing the same sweatshirt and pants, still had no makeup, but had an entirely different affect. She actually did the ritual, quite well: she did a floor bow to the altar, stepped over and bowed to me, bowed away, sat down and turned around, bowed again.

"Was that it?" she asked.

"Perfect. Where'd you learn?"

"I asked that dyke again. Told her I'd forgotten. She went over the whole thing. Actually took me out in the hallway. It was sweet."

Helen had been with us for years, lived right there in Somerville. She ran a tight ship.

"I'm not sure she's a dyke," Jess said.

"She is." Her partner lived with her, practiced with us also.

"Anyway, I'm sorry about yesterday. I was a bitch."

"All right."

"I was trying to do so well. I couldn't do anything."

"The harder you try, the worse you do. It's hard to persuade people of that."

"I'm still not doing well. Still haven't followed my first breath."

"It doesn't matter. It's the intention that's important."

"I have an intention?"

"Just the fact that you've come. You show up on the cushion."

"That's enough?"

"About 80 percent."

Her face had softened from the day before, still looked tired. Her eyes were soft and vulnerable. Not a bad thing.

"Did you come early today?" I asked. "You look tired."

"Am I a total hag?"

"You're beautiful." She was. Her face without all that hardware and paint, without that brittle quality, was lovely. "Your eyes just seem sleepy."

"I can't sleep. Happened again today. I woke up early. Figured I might as well come in."

All kinds of things interrupted sleep on retreat. It wasn't unusual.

"Though I don't know why," she said. "I can't meditate worth shit."

Her mouth twisted a little, and she looked down. Tears poured, just poured, from her eyes, and she started to sob.

"I miss my mother," she said.

I had done *dokusan* a number of times, and tears were not uncommon, especially on retreat, when people got worn down. But I had never seen someone break down so thoroughly as this. She wasn't loud, but her whole body shook. It went on and on.

"I'm sorry," she said, after a while.

"Don't be. You need to do this."

"You said that thing this morning. We block things with our body. That's what I've been doing. I knew it before you said it. I got here and was just too tired, couldn't block it anymore. I've been crying all day."

"That's great."

"The pain is totally gone from my ass. My back is better. I'm still a total wreck. Sore muscles all over the place. But I'm not holding it back."

"You shouldn't."

"Doesn't it disturb people?"

"I haven't heard a thing."

"I don't sob loud. But my body moves. I've been blowing my nose."

"How does that compare with traffic sounds, or noise from the playground?" There was a school playground a block away, and we'd been hearing boom boxes, vociferous basketball. "It's just sound. People deal with it."

"Crying's different. It's hard being around someone who's upset."

"Your meditation mat is your castle. What happens there is your business. Nobody's going to do anything."

"I'm not meditating."

"You're being present with your experience, doing what you need to. I spent a whole retreat crying about my father, and that was thirty years after he died. This is what's happening on your mat. Nobody's going to touch you."

"I wish they would."

"But that's the beauty of it. We're together and completely alone. Both things at once. It's the safest place imaginable."

"It's so lonely."

"It can feel that way. But once you get through that loneliness, you're connected to everyone. The loneliness connects you."

I was talking way past where Jess was. She might remember that years down the road. The important thing was that she cried.

"My mother was always there for me. I was such a little bitch."

"You were doing what you had to at the time. She understood."

"She kept offering herself and I turned her down. I was a cunt."

"You were making yourself your own person. Had to separate from her."

I had no idea what I was talking about, basically. I didn't even know her mother. At the same time, I was sure of everything I said. Retreats were like that.

"How am I going to get through this?" she asked.

"Just by doing it. You go on until it's over."

"It seems endless."

"Nothing's endless."

I could still remember the retreat where I'd cried for my father. Jake had been completely understanding, though I was talking about something that might as well have been in the dark ages. He made it completely natural.

Jess kept sobbing. Her whole body collapsed, she was shaking, all kinds of tension coming out. Finally she exhausted herself, sat straight. She took out a handkerchief and blew her nose.

"I'm a human snot machine," she said. "Got a bucket?"

"I have spare handkerchiefs."

"I brought three. Felt this coming on."

She wiped off her face with her hands, tried to straighten up.

"I'm a mess. I've been a total fucking mess the whole time you've known me. How do you put up with it?"

"I like it."

"Why?"

"I don't know. I just do."

She laughed again. "You're totally nuts." She put her hands together and bowed. "Is that what I do?"

"It's what everybody else does. I get tired of it, to be honest. We're not Japanese."

She laughed. "Now what do I do?"

"Continue."

"Go out there and cry?"

"If that's what happens. You're doing what you should be. Just be with what's going on."

"Maybe I'll even meditate a little."

"It could happen." Whatever meditation is.

"This is a strange activity."

"It's very strange, and very natural. People don't do it, but it's the most natural thing in the world. Also the sanest."

She bowed again, and I bowed back. "I'd like to kiss you," she said.

"You can kiss me when the retreat's over. Right now I'm your teacher. Show some respect."

She laughed.

If she'd kissed me right then I didn't know what might happen. We were as close as two human beings get.

"This is a kiss, then." She bowed.

I bowed back.

"It was better that we didn't do it. You were right."

We did do it, was the truth of the matter, just then, in that room. We'd been as intimate as if we had. We were lovers.

The practice was to be that way with the whole world.

16

THE FIRST THING I NOTICED the next day was that Jess was there at six. She stood out because her place was down the middle, with the room dividers, and she was the only one. Attendance fell after the weekend, though some people came before and after work. That morning she was the only one.

Maybe Sunday was her day off; she had gotten to bed early and gotten enough sleep. She seemed to sit well.

The next thing I noticed was that she wasn't there when the talk began.

I was looking for her. She was my touchstone, I had realized the day before, the person I taught to. You teach to everyone, but she had caught me short that first day, asking me to start at the beginning. That was important. You couldn't assume anything.

I also felt close to her emotionally, Kevin as well. He would serve as a substitute.

I couldn't help wondering where she was.

The other thing that threw me that morning was that Jake had me do the bows. We'd gone to the *dokusan* room, where we picked up the incense, and he said, "I've got it," in the most casual way. It wasn't until he had the lighted incense and was walking out that I realized what was happening. He was making me the speaker.

The day before I had thought he should. Today I wasn't so sure.

Then I wasn't sure what happened when the talk began. We sat in our places in the front, but if I was the officiating priest I should be starting, though I had no idea what to talk about. I was waiting for him.

For a long time he said nothing. The day before, I thought he'd shown no signs of his problem—though I didn't know what happened when he wasn't talking, which was most of the time. But now he seemed to be having a spell, wore an absolutely absent gaze. I looked for Madeleine, but she was looking down, avoiding my eyes.

"Jake?" I said.

"I had something and lost it," he said. "Give me a minute."

"I can go ahead." Though I didn't know with what.

"No. Wait a minute."

We sat for what must have been three or four minutes. People had assumed their best posture. If we'd sat the whole time in silence it would have been good enough for me.

Finally Jake said, "The Buddha held up a flower and Mahakashyapa smiled." He turned to me.

As he said those words I realized what the moment in the *dokusan* room had been. It was what the whole retreat had been, the whole week. My whole life with him for that matter. I was to talk about transmission.

It's one of the most famous stories in Zen, supposedly the founding story, though it may be apocryphal and created by someone to make a point. A huge group of monks were sitting in front of the Buddha, waiting for him to deliver a lecture. For a long time he didn't say anything, then he held up a flower. One monk, Mahakashyapa, smiled. One out of twelve hundred got the point.

The whole of the Buddha's message could be reduced to that: do you appreciate this flower? Do you see that it contains the whole universe? One monk did, and he became the model for Zen transmission, which is outside the scriptures, just one mind connecting to another, beyond words.

If you want to study the ineffable, it's right in front of you. A leaf on a tree is ineffable. If you want to know the creator, look around, he's everywhere. If you want to know eternity, this is it. This moment is as eternal as they come. The answer is not in a book. It's not in a talk. It's right there in front of you. Look.

The problem with this subject—which by its whole nature is somewhat opposed to talking—is that it was full of emotion for me. Jake had just done with a simple physical gesture what he was asking me to talk about, did it in a way that spoke volumes. Then he seemed to have forgotten the whole point—which tore me up in another way—and come back just enough to say one thing. The Buddha held up a flower and Mahakashyapa smiled.

What I wanted to talk about was the millions of ways Jake had embodied that for me, from the first day I met him and he stood there smiling while Josh pitched an adolescent fit until that simple gesture of stepping in front of me and taking the incense, with everything in between: taking us to a pizza parlor after Josh's fit so we could have a little food and calm down; listening to me with a modest smile as if he hadn't done anything while I tried to express my gratitude; taking me as a student as if there were nothing more normal than a half-assed high school history teacher moving to Bar Harbor for eight weeks to study Zen; showing me how to sit and sitting with me patiently through days and nights that turned into years.

Riding with him on the Mount Desert bike paths through months of summers; watching him take a whole bike apart and put it back together as if he were doing nothing, as if there were no time involved at all, when he knew the owner would come steaming in at five demanding it back; watching him eat pancakes at the diner, lobster rolls from a roadside stand, some goofball donut from a Chinese donut shop as if it were the finest French pastry in the world.

The man was there. In everything he did, he was right there. Even when he sat waiting for his mind to return, which he knew it might never do, he was there. It was so true that I could take it for granted. I did. I ignored a teaching that was right in front of me.

I totally screwed up the talk. In thinking about this man who was constantly present, but whom I couldn't talk about because he literally was present, I was entirely un-present, patching together a talk by remembering things I'd read. I told stories from the Zen tradition, some of which everyone had heard multiple times, but they were all dead because I couldn't talk about the thing that was alive for me in the moment. I was sweating bullets as I spoke, pausing for long stretches of time, starting one story and abandoning it for another, getting two stories confused, forgetting the names of characters.

It was a disaster. By the time it was over Madeleine was staring at the floor in embarrassment, Kevin had had his eyes completely shut—sleeping?—for a good fifteen minutes, and everyone else was shifting in their places. For the second straight day, a record, no one had questions. They all just wished I would shut the fuck up.

So much for this particular act of transmission.

When we walked up the stairs during the after-lunch break, Jake stepped into my room. The kindest thing he could have done was take out a gun and blow my brains out.

"What happened to Jessica?" he asked.

"I don't know. She was here early, then left."

"How's she been in *dokusan*?"

"Her usual self. All over the place. She got into mourning for her mother, who died a few months ago. Did a lot of crying yesterday."

Jake reddened, frowned.

"Maybe she was crying too much," I said, "and she was afraid she'd disturb people. She worried about that yesterday."

"There are ways to deal with that."

"I know."

"She could sit in a separate room. One of us could sit with her."

"I told her everything was fine yesterday. I honestly hadn't noticed the crying. I didn't see her go out this morning. She just suddenly wasn't there."

Jake nodded, headed out the door.

"I'm sorry about that talk, Jake."

"Why?"

"I screwed up. All over the place."

"I've heard worse. The point isn't a polished performance."

That was a good thing.

"You talk from your gut. Sometimes it's twisted up." For sure. "You give people what you've got."

I skipped work period that day—usually I took one of the jobs—and took a long walk around the neighborhood, trying to get rid of that feeling. It wasn't happening. My longing for some real exercise, a swim, was almost palpable. Finally I saw I just had to sit with it. I'd been telling people that for three days.

Madeleine came to *dokusan* late that afternoon.

"I really think I'd like to see Jake," she said. "I've waited long enough."

"He doesn't want to see anyone," I said.

I had no idea why I said that. It just sounded right.

"Don't you think he'd see me?"

"I'm sure he would. But he doesn't want to see anyone."

"Couldn't you ask him?"

"I could. I'm just trying to decide on the right thing to do." For her, I meant. She thought I meant for him.

"We can think about that together," I said.

She sat there staring at me. Tears came to her eyes.

"It's as if he's not here," she said. "It's as if he's dead."

"He's here. He's just not talking."

"What good is he to me if he's not talking?"

I didn't say anything for a moment. "I think it's some good," I said.

"I've never sat so long in my life. If this were Maine, I would long since have gone on a business trip."

I didn't see the point. Couldn't she leave for a business trip from here?

"I'll get him if you want me to," I said.

"Didn't I say I wanted you to?"

"If you want me to now."

The tears ran down her face. She really needed to bawl. She wouldn't do it in front of me.

"All right then." She looked as if she'd like to smack me. "Don't get him. What am I supposed to do?"

I thought the answer to that was obvious. Go sit on your cushion.

"I'll be any help I can, Madeleine," I said.

She skipped the bow, stood up and walked out.

Then she came back, stood at the door, and bowed. I bowed back.

She would happily have killed me. But she would have bowed first.

At the end of the evening, we do one final service with no bells whatsoever. The lights are dim, and we do three floor bows, then chant the Refuges. It always seems a perfect end to the day. I walk to my room ready for sleep.

That evening, when we got to the top of the stairs, Jake said, "I want to check on Jessica."

"You want to call?"

"I want to go down there. I want to see her."

If his spells could have given him a crazy idea, I would have thought this was one. I almost held my hand to his forehead.

"You want to walk?"

"There's a cab stand a block away."

"Shouldn't we change?"

"I'd rather not take the time."

He was heading for the Green Street Grill in his robes? He'd cause a sensation.

"You don't need to come if you don't want," he said. "I just want to talk to her."

"I'm coming."

I sure as hell wasn't going to let him go out there alone.

Jake was right; there was a cab stand a block away. I'd never noticed. The cabbie didn't seem surprised at a couple of Zen priests in robes—this was Cambridge, after all—but did raise an eyebrow when we said where we were going.

When we arrived, Jake told him we'd be coming back— "You just having a quick one?" the cabbie asked—but that he didn't know how long we'd be. The cabbie said he'd be at the Mass. Ave. cab stand. We gave him a nice tip since it had been a short trip.

The bar—I shouldn't have been surprised—was dead at that point on a Monday. I was glad our crowd of barflies didn't stay there for five or six hours every evening. Jess was cleaning up, washing glasses, when we came in.

"Holy shit," she said. "Padre. You guys are checking up."

"Just wondering how you are," Jake said. "We were worried."

"Jake always likes a beer or two in the middle of a retreat," I said.

"You can't blame him," Jess said. "The usual?"

"I'm going to pass," Jake said. "You go ahead," he said to me.

"I'd like some tonic water," I said. "Hold the gin."

The truth—it's hard to explain, as difficult as retreat can be—is that the last thing you want is alcohol. You don't want what clarity you have even slightly fogged over. On a normal day, I find a beer relaxing. On retreat it would be intrusive. I have no taste for it.

The tonic water didn't take a minute. Jess knew her way around.

"So we were worried," Jake said. "Neither of us saw you go."

"You thought I'd crapped out."

"It happens," Jake said. "I once took a hike in the middle of *sesshin*."

"Hank told me," Jess said.

That was during one of our morning talks, which Jake didn't know about. He didn't seem to notice.

"I wasn't taking a walk," Jess said. "And I wasn't crapping out. Maybe Hank told you, I had a rough first day."

"It goes without saying," Jake said.

"The second wasn't a cakewalk either. Even this morning, I was still sore. Kind of tired. Still couldn't follow a breath if you'd held a gun to my head."

Jake laughed.

"But something yesterday made me see what this is all about," she said. "Just the tiniest glimpse, though I still have no idea what I'm doing. Not one clue how to meditate."

"No one knows that," Jake said.

"I'm still at the point where I think I'll figure it out."

Jess was deeper than she looked.

"Anyway," she said. "I decided yesterday I want to do this. I want to learn what it is, however long it takes. I want Hank to be my teacher."

I actually blushed. I thought she preferred Jake. It was just as well she hadn't heard the talk that day.

"He's taken a lot of shit from me," she said. "But he's hung in there. I left today because I had to cry. I'd been holding back, but this morning I knew I had to cut loose. So after breakfast I came back and sat in my apartment. I have a cushion there, Padre. I bought one."

"Great."

"I sat on that thing and bawled my eyes out. Sobbing and

moaning. Pretty soon I was lying on the floor, rolling around. I had to do it. I knew I did. Get it all out."

It probably wasn't all out. It took time.

"Did I do the right thing?" Jess asked.

"We could have found you a place in the house," Jake said. "But you have good instincts."

Jess beamed. She loved being praised by this man.

He turned to me. "I'd like to talk to Jess alone for a while."

That surprised me. Jake spent plenty of time talking to students alone, in *dokusan* and elsewhere; I was in no way privy to everything that went on. But Jess wasn't his student. She had just said she wanted to work with me. And he'd never talked to her privately. I couldn't imagine what he wanted to say.

I nodded, smiled, took my tonic water and walked to a table away from the bar.

They talked for half an hour. I had to admit to a slight feeling of paranoia, wondering if Jake was asking about our meetings ("He was really good, Padre. He only grabbed my tits once"), but it didn't seem like that kind of conversation. Not that I was looking or anything. But I couldn't help seeing out of the corner of my eye, and Jess got more and more involved, radiant in the way only Jake could make her feel. He did most of the talking.

Finally, when they were finished, he called me over.

"I think we should have a drink," Jess said. "On the house." She looked back toward the kitchen. "Not that the house is going to know."

I looked at Jake. I'd follow his lead.

"Maybe just a swallow for us," Jake said. "It really doesn't go with sitting." He turned to me. "Can you take a swallow?"

"Just one."

Jess got out three shot glasses and took a bottle from behind the bar. "Jose Cuervo tequila," she said. "My favorite."

She gave us both a small swallow in the bottom of the glass, herself a full shot.

"To clear minds," she said. "Even when they're fuzzy." This woman knew more than I thought. "And to the truth, which will set us free."

"May all beings be free," Jake said.

We clinked glasses, and I drank my swallow of tequila, which I was not used to. Even that little bit burned. Jess knocked her whole shot back.

I had no idea what this was all about.

"Good night, Padre," she said. She leaned over the bar and kissed him on the mouth. "See you in the morning."

"We won't check on you again," Jake said.

"I also get to kiss my teacher," Jess said. "Since we're not in that little room."

She kissed me on the mouth too.

"Expect me bright and early, boys," she said. "I'm rarin' to go."

"It's important to get rest," I said.

"I can't sleep anyway," she said.

"Maybe tonight you will," I said. It was the stuff about her mother that woke her up.

"After that shot, I'd be asleep in ten minutes," Jake said.

"I'm used to it, Padre."

"Don't get too used to it."

She blew us a kiss as we stepped out the door.

Our cabbie was still at the stand. He was the only one. He must have wondered where we'd been.

"After that first one," he said, "the second goes down mighty smooth."

"You said it," Jake said.

We rode in silence for a minute or two. Jake was gazing out the window, his face reflected in the streetlights.

Finally he said, "You'd have told me if something happened."

"What did she say?" I asked.

"Nothing. That isn't what we talked about."

I was glad to hear it. I pondered his question.

"It's a moot point," I said. "Nothing was going to happen."

"I guess that's right," he said. "It is a moot point."

We rode on a while longer.

"It was a stupid question," he said. "I'm sorry."

It wasn't a stupid question. I don't know what the real answer was. But I somehow felt that—though I was just as attracted to sex as ever—I wouldn't have a problem with it again. The attraction was there, and would stay there, but not as a problem.

When we begin, we imagine that someday, if we practice long and hard enough, all of our problems will be gone. Every aspect of our conditioning that gives us trouble will disappear, wiped out by the power of *zazen*.

Our problems don't disappear. If they did, we'd lose touch with humanity. They don't go anywhere. But we know them well. We know all their tricks. We don't act on them.

Except for occasionally grabbing a hot babe by the tits.

"You guys take care now," the cabbie said as he dropped us off at what he probably assumed was a monastery. "I appreciate you taking care of me." We'd given another large tip. "I never seen where you went."

"We knew we could count on you," I said.

Inside, all the lights were off, and people were camped out in sleeping bags all over. We had to tiptoe up the stairs. When we got to the top, Jake turned and bowed. "Thanks for coming," he said.

"It was my pleasure," I said.

It was a short night at that point, but I had punched through to where I wasn't sleeping much and woke up at four thirty completely refreshed. I stayed in bed until the wake-up bell, got up and did some stretching, got dressed in my robes. When I went to get Jake a little before six his lights were still off, and he was in bed. I hadn't heard him stirring, should have come in sooner. I didn't want to waken him with the light, so I walked over and put my hand on his shoulder. I stood there in bewilderment for a few minutes, not taking it in, before I realized he was dead.

17

SOME YEARS BACK Jake gave a talk about a teacher who predicted the time of his death or died exactly when he wanted to; I don't remember which. The question was, did he bring about his death because he felt that was the time, or was he so attuned to his body that he knew when it would happen? There were those two possibilities, Jake said, and he wasn't sure what the answer was. They amounted to the same thing.

I would give a great deal of thought to that matter in the days and weeks that followed Jake's death, all the ways I should have seen it coming. There were a million hints, right up to that last evening. But when it finally happened, it hit me like a freight train, actually knocked me to the floor, if crumpling slowly and awkwardly into a sitting position constitutes being knocked. It took the breath out of me. I sat there as if everything had been vaporized, the whole world had disappeared; that was how alone I felt. I had no idea what to do. I wasn't sure I even *could* stand.

But I had to. I was in charge, people were downstairs waiting; it was time for the sitting to begin. The way things are in Soto Zen, with everyone facing the wall, the only person who would know Jake wasn't there was the timekeeper, who rang bells to mark the ritual.

I took the incense myself, offered it and did three floor bows, walked around the zendo in the morning *jundo*, people doing *gassho* in greeting. All they heard were the footsteps behind them. My legs were like jelly as I did the bows and walked. I wasn't sure from one step to the next I could make it, but did get back to my cushion, made the bows that preceded my sitting down.

The timekeeper looked puzzled, but that's the way Zen is: come hell or high water, the sitting starts at six. If no priest had come they still would have sat. I didn't actually sit down, went and got Madeleine from her place, closed the door and walked her down the hall.

"Jake is dead, Madeleine," I said. "He died last night in his sleep. He's lying up in bed."

Her mouth dropped and she slammed her hand to it. I grabbed and held her, held her up—I could feel her going down the same way I had—then she started to shake and sob. I held her through that; we were shaking together. Finally I walked her into the kitchen, which I should have done in the first place, and told Darcy.

"Holy Mother of God," she said. She crossed herself. "We've got to call an ambulance."

"I don't want them screeching up here like it's an emergency," I said. "I know he's dead. He's been dead a while."

"You can tell them that," she said. "But they've still got to come."

"Can you do it?" I said. "I think I should tell the group."

"Tell the group?" Madeleine asked. "Now?"

All this was moving so fast that I hardly knew what to do. It was rare to let anything interrupt a Zen *sesshin*. I'd never known it to happen. I once heard of a group in California that sat through a small earthquake. But when the teacher had died, when that was suddenly a new fact in the world, it seemed to me the students had a right to know. You didn't wait for some ideal moment to tell them. You told them now.

"I think they would resent it if I waited," I said.

"What will we do?" Madeleine said. "About the whole thing?"

"I don't know. We'll just have to see. But I think I should tell them."

"I can call the ambulance," Darcy said. "I'll tell them to keep quiet."

"People are going to need breakfast sooner or later," I said. "I don't know when."

"It'll keep," Darcy said.

I said all those words, but didn't know where they came from. I seemed to be taking care of things, making sense, but actually I was a zombie. It hadn't hit me yet. It had knocked me to the ground, but hadn't blown me out of the room.

I hugged Madeleine again. It was obvious that, hard as this news was for her, the thought of giving it to the group terrified her.

It terrified me too. But I had to do it.

I walked down the hallway and into the zendo. Already that door had opened and closed more than it did most mornings, and here I was opening it again. People pick up on things like that, especially by the third day. There was also the whole vibe of the house, which I knew some people must feel.

I walked to my place, sat down and faced the group. I still had no idea what I was going to say. My body was churning with energy, a huge weight in the pit of my stomach.

"Would everyone please turn around?" I said.

My voice sounded weak and rough. Not everyone heard, I'm sure. But the instruction passed around the room body by body, as people turned to face me. The group looked solemn, and puzzled. It could only be bad news.

I waited until everyone was still, waited a little longer, then spoke.

"Many of you know that Jake had health problems in recent years," I said. "Problems with his memory, as well as his heart and circulation. But they didn't fundamentally change how he was in the world, his zest for life, his devotion to his students. He wanted to have this *sesshin* though he didn't feel up to giving talks or doing *dokusan*."

I took a long slow breath, let it out.

"Jake died last night in his sleep," I said. There was a gasp from the group, like a hushed shout. They gaped at me. "I found him this morning on my way to come down here. It was like he was resting." But so still and cold, stiff to the touch. He had been dead a long time. "I think we need to talk," I said. "I know we need to talk. But I think for a while we should sit without talking. Sit with this new fact, try to take it in." A few people started to turn, but I said, "Let's sit like this. Let's face the center."

People straightened their posture, sat more formally.

"We'll sit until the end of the first period," I said.

I said all that spontaneously because I knew, as soon as I spoke, that I wasn't ready for talking. It had been only a matter of minutes since I'd discovered his body, and I'd been doing things the whole time. I needed to stop for a while. In all of our practice, *zazen* was the central action, what we did first, last, and always, our way of dealing with everything. It was what Jake had done when he needed to deal with difficulty. We needed to too.

People were sobbing all over the room, wiping their eyes and blowing their noses. It wasn't a silent sitting and wasn't especially still, but we kept coming back to that one fact, the one we had to see. It wasn't going anywhere.

Forty minutes wouldn't be enough to absorb it.

What I kept thinking of was his determination to see Jess

the night before, his last act as a teacher. He had known we'd been seeing each other, had seen us together at least that one time, and wanted to check up on her, and on me. He got some peace about that at the end. I was glad he could put it to rest.

I thought of that last bow we made to each other, outside the rooms. I wondered if he knew it was the last one.

People die in their sleep, we say: he went peacefully, he never knew, but I wonder about that. People often awaken just before they die, one last moment of lucidity, and I wondered if Jake had done that the night before. I wondered if it was a frightening moment, an exalted moment, a sad one. I wished I could have been there for it, after all we'd been through together. I wished I could have been with him.

But I also thought he would have wanted to be alone. He was the most comfortable with solitude of anyone I've ever met, with solitude and with crowds, and I thought he would have wanted to be alone for that moment so he could take it in. He had loved life and—if it makes any sense to say, about that inconceivable state—would love death too, and the transition in between. He totally absorbed himself in whatever he did.

At the end of forty minutes the bell rang. It seemed like ten. I needed more time, much more, but I had the group to think about too.

"Let's not walk," I said. "Let's just stand and stretch our legs. Then gather in a group, the way we do for a talk."

Some people were still sobbing, but most had cried themselves out for the moment. They blew their noses, wiped their eyes. They gathered their cushions and moved into a semicircle.

I sat back down. One by one they did too. I waited until they were still.

While we had been sitting, I'd heard the men come to get the body. Now I noticed them moving by the door, carrying it out. I was glad. People might have wanted to see it, but I wasn't sure how that would go. There would be time for viewing later.

"I know we need a lot more time with this," I said. "I for one need to sit more. I'm not sure what to do. But I thought we need to talk. People must be full of words."

"I don't think we should continue *sesshin*," Helen said, the woman who had been in charge. "I don't think I can. I'm too upset."

"I agree," someone else said.

"There's a tradition of sitting *sesshin* after the teacher dies," someone else said. "I think we should honor that."

"We can decide," I said. "We can decide all that. Right now I think we should talk, about how we're feeling, what we're thinking, whatever we want. Not necessarily some big statement about what Jake meant to you. There'll be time for that. Just whatever is on your mind."

While I was talking, Madeleine came in and took her place. I assumed that meant the ambulance people had left, or that Darcy was taking care of things.

"I'm in shock," someone said. "Literally. I can't feel a thing. I knew Jake was sick, knew he was getting older, but he seemed so alive. Always so alive. It's as if he *was* life. I can't imagine life without him."

Heads were nodding all over the room. I couldn't help noticing that, right in the middle, Jess was still crying. Tears still soaked her cheeks. She was in the middle of the group, but didn't seem part of them. She continued to weep after the others had finished, looking down.

Madeleine noticed too. She was sitting beside her, had her arm around her.

The conversation continued, and I felt sure it had been the right thing to do. People needed to talk with that emotion; words were pouring out after two days of silence. They were saying what Jake meant to them, telling stories about him,

talking about the first time they'd met him, the most important thing he'd said to them. It was like the talking people
always do after *sesshin*, but all around this one subject. In the
middle of it, there was a long pause, waiting for someone to
continue, and Jess spoke.

"Jake was"—she spoke slowly—"like, my father. I called
him Padre the first time I met him, it just seemed so right, he
looked like a little priest. But then as I got to know him, and
he kept coming to see me, I realized he really was my father,
and that was why he was coming. I was calling him the right
thing."

I understood how people could exaggerate in such situations, but I also thought Jess had cracked a little. Nobody in
the group—most of whom had sat together for years—had
even so much as seen her before; she'd been a Zen student for
a matter of days, and now she was saying this, crying all the
while? I thought she'd completely lost it.

"You mean he was like a father to you," Helen said.

"He was my father," Jess said.

"You mean . . ." Helen said.

"He was her father," Madeleine said. "He'd been estranged
from her mother for years, hadn't ever gotten to know his
daughter, her mother didn't want that, but her mother died
in June. She's lost two parents just like that." She gave Jess
a squeeze. "But Jake came to see her. It was a lot of why he
came to Cambridge at all. To meet his daughter."

Talk about a shock. Now my mouth was gaping, I hope not
literally. It had been right there before me, and I hadn't even
seen it.

"He got to meet his daughter before he died," Madeleine
said. "He was so happy about that."

"Last night he came to say good-bye," Jess said. "I didn't
know at the time, but now I see that's what it was. It had gotten to be this little joke between us, both of us knowing but

not quite saying the punch line. I could hardly believe it when he finally did, I was so happy. Last night he came to see me, just to talk about my mother."

"Where?" somebody asked.

"I'm a barmaid at the Green Street Grill," Jess said.

"Jake went to a bar in the middle of *sesshin*?" somebody said. "That's perfect."

The whole crowd burst into laughter. They'd needed to.

"He didn't drink anything," Jess said. "Just a little tequila."

Another roar of laughter.

"He just started talking about her," Jess said. "About my mother when she was young, before I was born. What she was like, and how hard she practiced, what a deep person she was, how stubborn she was. All that was exactly like her, the same person. It was amazing to hear somebody telling me all that, which I already knew but also didn't know. He told me how much he loved my mother, how glad he was to have made this beautiful daughter, how happy he was to have met me. He'd wanted to all my life."

The whole week suddenly looked different. I'd had no idea what was going on. I felt like an idiot.

"He was saying good-bye to me, but I didn't know. Now I wonder if he knew. But I think he did. I think he knew."

I thought he did too.

"It's a sobering thought," Helen said.

The whole group seemed stunned by this news. It was a fact—perhaps a shocking fact to some—that they had just learned about their teacher, who had also just died, and couldn't speak for himself. I wished he were there. But in that vacuum, in the long silence that followed Helen's remark, Madeleine began to speak.

"This was back in the old days," she said, "twenty years ago, when Jake was starting to teach. There were just a few of us, a handful of summer people up in Bar Harbor. Jake struck up a relationship with one of the women, her name was Olivia, though her middle name was Paige. That was what she called herself later, after Jessica was born, in what must have seemed a new stage of her life." She smoothed Jessica's hair in the back.

"Anyway, I wanted it to be me, but he started seeing Olivia. It was a real meeting of minds, deep minds, they met at a very deep place. She was a natural at meditation, which I certainly was not, and I'm not sure anyone has been since. Maybe Hank."

"Not by a long shot," I said.

"I think he imagined eventually teaching with her. Saw her as a life partner, in every sense. They were deeply involved, that word *deep* keeps coming up, but not for a terribly long time. A matter of months. When she got pregnant, with this beautiful young woman, he hesitated. He was making no money, living hand to mouth. I had started to support him and the practice place. I guess he thought I might stop if he married another woman. Maybe I would have been that petty, who knows? I hadn't known him a terribly long time myself.

"Olivia, about as intuitive a person as ever lived, felt him hesitate, and took off. She wanted him to jump right in. But she also valued him as a teacher, didn't want him to stop teaching. And she knew she was more drawn to women, which had been true all her life. It really was as if their minds had come together more than their bodies. Something beyond physical attraction."

Though that had been there too, I was sure.

"For some reason she had to wipe that part of her life out forever," Madeleine said, "not even see Jake, not let him know their daughter. I didn't understand that, though I respected it. She didn't much want to know me either. But I followed her from afar, followed her career, and when she died this year, I let him know. Managed to find out where this young woman was working."

"How'd you do that?" Jess asked.

"I went to the funeral, spoke to some people afterward. Actually came down for a drink one day myself. That's quite a crowd."

"Bunch of beer drunks. I know."

"But that's the real reason, which I have found quite hard to admit, that we had the *sesshin* here this year. It wasn't that Jake decided to move to Cambridge and start a practice place, as I managed to convince myself. It wasn't that he thought he'd be here for months or years.

"He would have had *sesshin* anyway. He wanted to see his students one more time. But he came down here to see his daughter. That's why we're here right now."

It was true. That was what the whole thing was about. The whole trip was an excuse to spend time at the Green Street Grill.

While Madeleine had been talking, actually for the past fifteen minutes or so, I had been aware that someone was standing outside the door. I thought it must be Darcy, worried about breakfast, and couldn't understand why she didn't just come in. She wasn't shy. But the conversation seemed to have stopped, so I stepped away, and went to the door.

It was Lily from the Golden Donut, holding two shopping bags.

"Hank," she said. "I bring donuts."

"You brought donuts?"

"Jake say bring donuts fourth day. Time his students need treat. Get over hump. I walk here from Central Square, find ambulance, take Jake away. They tell me Jake die last night. I no believe."

"He did, Lily. He died in his sleep."

I put my arms around her. Tears were pouring down her cheeks.

The Jake Knew He Was Going to Die meter jumped up another notch. This was looking weird. On the other hand, I couldn't believe he'd want donuts served after he was gone. He would have wanted to be there.

I stepped back into the room and spoke.

"I think we should have breakfast now. We'll have a regular *oryoki* breakfast. But before we do, Jake had arranged a treat for us. I'd like the servers to stay for it."

Everyone took their places around the room, facing the center, and Lily, tears still streaming down her face, went around serving donuts from two boxes. We put them on the napkins we had left over from tea. After Lily made the rounds, I had her sit beside me, and take one for herself. We bowed, and began to eat.

"This was Jake's favorite treat at Lily's diner," I said.

It was the chocolate cake donuts with chocolate icing. They were amazing, though rather rich.

He had definitely planned to be there.

Afterward—though we hardly needed it—we ate our oatmeal in the big bowl and stewed fruit in the small one. We were full at the end of that breakfast, full the way Jake liked to be. I don't know how we'd have done meditating on it.

People had learned a lot about their teacher that morning, much that they hadn't known. I wasn't sure how they were doing. But the last gift the teacher gives, and it is the hardest for some to accept, is to let us know he is human. The last gift he gives—it's a precious one—is to die.

When the Buddha was dying, and Ananda and the others had to face that, that was the final teaching, the thing he had insisted on all his life. All conditioned things are impermanent, and your teacher, like you, is an impermanent being. You have the same capacity to free yourself he did. Be a lamp unto yourselves.

At the end of the meal, I said, "Helen's right about *sesshin*. There's too much to process, too much to absorb." Especially now. "People need to talk. Though sitting is the best way to absorb all this. I'll talk it over with Madeleine, but I think we should prepare a service for Friday, right here. It was going to be the last day of *sesshin*. It gives us a chance to gather our thoughts, and prepare to say good-bye."

I bowed to the group. They bowed to me, began filing out.

As I would discover three days later, the group absorbed the new information well. They knew Jake was human; it was what they most loved about him, that he was so obviously human yet also full of compassion and wisdom. A huge crowd showed up for the service, all kinds of people from Mount Desert. It was a solemn and raucous affair, a Buddhist funeral that I conducted—my first ever—followed by stories about Jake, laughing and crying. It lasted three hours.

I didn't know that on the Tuesday Jake died. I wasn't sure how they'd react. When the group filed out of the room, they immediately moved to the hallway, and outside on the sidewalk, to talk. Only Jess and I were left.

It wasn't that she was being shunned. People wanted to know her, to hear about Jake and her mother, but they also didn't want to overwhelm her. She was still slightly isolated.

She walked up and we hugged for a long time.

"I'm really going to need you now," she said. "I feel cut loose."

"I'm here."

"I really want to do this. In a way my mother never did. She didn't have a group."

"Right."

"I talked to Jake last night about how my mother was. How I always wanted to be like her, so disciplined, so devoted, kind of like a nun, with her music.

"Jake told me I wasn't supposed to be like her, I was supposed to be like me. *Zazen* would make me more like me. God knows what that is. I'm going to drink and fuck more?"

I shrugged. "Who knows?"

"Anyway, he said you could help me, in a way he never could. A father couldn't help his daughter. Another teacher could."

"You teach yourself. A teacher helps you."

"You've got to keep me on the straight and narrow. Keep me at it."

That sounded like a hell of a task.

"Stay in touch, anyway. You've got to be with me."

"I will. And you've got to promise to stay out of my pants. I can't do that alone."

"Really? You seem like the Rock of Gibraltar."

"I'm a pebble in a stream. We've got to agree on that."

"It's a deal." She shook my hand. "Right now I feel like a walk. Want to come?"

"I better do some things here. I'll come to the bar tonight. We'll make plans."

"Sounds good."

We hugged, walked into the hall.

People were packing up sleeping bags, getting things together.

I walked upstairs looking for Madeleine. She was in Jake's room, putting away his belongings, crying.

"It still smells like him," she said. "The room smells like him, and his robes."

It was true. There was always a scent of incense around Jake, because he lit it every time he sat, even at home. You could smell it in the room.

I helped her get the things together. His suitcase was virtually packed. He'd been living out of it, quite neatly.

"Did that sound all right for the memorial service?" I asked. "I didn't mean to speak up without asking."

"It's fine."

"I didn't want to leave things open-ended."

"Everything you did this morning seemed right. But I think we need to talk about"—she waved her hand—"all this." She gestured to the room, meant the whole building.

"Is this the time?"

"It might not be. But if I wait, it's going to be harder."

"All right."

She sat in a chair in the corner, I on the edge of the bed.

"I don't think you should go through with it," she said. "I don't think you should run the center."

I had a terrific sinking sensation when she said that, as if I would fall if I weren't already sitting. It was almost as much of a shock as finding Jake dead. In a way it was related. Everything was disappearing. The world turned upside down.

"Really?" I said.

Funny that I would have gotten so attached to something I hadn't even thought about a week before.

"I've been thinking since I realized Jake's plan. That he had no intention of taking the center. He wanted it for you."

"Yes."

"I respect that wish. I feel bad about going against something he clearly wanted. But my idea was to have a place for him. A place where he could teach, meet students on a regular basis. A repository for his teaching. I wasn't interested in starting a center."

I nodded.

"You don't have the following he had. How could you? You haven't taught much. I don't know that all his students will want to be with you. In a way, you'll be starting from scratch. I don't know that you could support a center."

"Jake thought I could."

"Jake loved you. He was trying to take care of you."

That did it. I put my head down and started bawling.

Madeleine reached across and took my hand. She came and sat on the side of the bed, held me while I cried.

As difficult as it was for me to hear her words, there was truth to them. I hadn't taught much, hadn't given many talks. I hadn't often led services, though I would be leading a terribly important one in a couple of days. Jake had started to realize all that in the past week. He'd regretted not bringing me along sooner.

I didn't know that his students would study with me. They hardly knew me. Madeleine for one wouldn't be my student. It was hard to take a teacher seriously when you'd been to bed with him, even twenty years before.

The only student I had for sure was Jess. And she'd been practicing for less than a week.

"I'm not crying because of what you said," I managed to say after a while. "I just miss Jake. I realize how much I miss him."

"I know."

I had liked the idea of having a center. It would give me security, make Josh feel better about my situation. But there was a reason Jake had avoided it for so long, finally escaped it with his death. There was something fundamentally false in that security.

Madeleine had made the right decision. I wasn't ready.

"Have you seen Jake's will?" she asked.

"I haven't."

"He left you the house on Mount Desert. He told me last week."

In all that had been happening, I'd forgotten about it.

"He thought you should sell it," she said. "Or give it back to me. Assuming you'd be down here. But I think you should start all over. Start the way Jake did."

Put out flyers in the bike shop. Maybe I could even learn to work on bikes.

Forget it. Even Jake couldn't teach me that.

Maybe I could learn to flip pancakes.

"The place needs some work," she said.

"It does."

"And you've got to pay taxes. You've got to make enough to pay property tax every year."

Maybe I'd have to dust off the old teacher's certificate.

That wouldn't be bad. I'd have the summers free.

"I hope you understand," she said.

"I do."

She was Jake's student, Jake's benefactor. She wasn't mine.

"I want you to stay until the memorial service, of course," she said. "As long after that as you need."

"They still have my room at the Y."

"Don't be silly."

We finished getting Jake's things together, and I went next door and changed out of my robes, walked downstairs. The crowd seemed to have cleared out, all the sleeping bags gone. I figured I'd take a walk, maybe drop in at the bookstore and let Morrie know. Jake had had lots of friends in Cambridge.

Kevin was sitting on the front stoop, staring at the traffic. He only wore a light shirt, held his arms folded around himself, shivering. He needed a sweater.

"Hello, Hank," he said. "Bad day."

"Bad day," I said. The teaching was that every day was a good day, but it was hard to see that now. I pulled him up from where he was sitting, gave him a hug.

He was the one person all day who hadn't been crying. He still had those sad eyes, looked terribly discouraged, but couldn't bring himself to cry. It was as if he always expected some disaster, this event confirmed his general view of things.

"I don't know what to do with myself," he said. "I've got these days off from work."

"I know."

"Is it okay to sit some more? Will they let me sit in there?"

"It's always fine to sit. I'm sure they will."

I wasn't sure who this "they" was.

Kevin was the one person I might have urged to do less sitting.

"I've been wanting to talk to you," he said. "I was going to do *dokusan* today."

"I was just going to walk for a while. You want to walk?"

"Sure."

"You need a sweater? Get a sweater."

Somebody had to act like his mother.

When he came back out we walked down Hampshire, taking our time.

"That talk you gave yesterday," he said. "Knowing your teacher through his body. Learning by just being around him. I didn't really understand."

"That talk was kind of a mess," I said.

The thought occurred to me that, if that talk had been better, Madeleine might have let me take over the center.

"It stuck with me, though," he said. "I can't seem to get it out of my mind."

He didn't seem to have heard me.

"It's as if I got it in some deep place," he said. "I got it in my body, but don't have it in my head yet."

It must have been a deep place, for him to get that talk.

"Anyway," he said. "I liked Jake. He was a great guy. And of course I'm sad he's dead. But he never really spoke to me. Maybe he was too old. Or I'm immature. But that talk of yours really got me, like no talk ever has. It made me want to do this. Really practice Zen."

"That's great," I said. It was a miracle.

"And I never thought I'd say this to anybody. It sounds cheesy or something. I hope it's okay. But I want you to be my teacher."

We stopped, turned to face each other. He was blushing, looking down.

"That probably sounds stupid," he said.

"It's not stupid. I'm honored."

"I'm not sure what it means."

"It is rather mysterious."

"I don't know how we start."

"I think we already started."

"Yeah. I guess that's right." He shrugged.

"I don't suppose you know how to repair bikes," I said.

"No. What? You got a bike down?"

"It was just an idea."

"I'm a total klutz around tools. A hopeless case."

"Me too. How about flipping pancakes?"

"*Pancakes?* Jesus. I never did it."

"We'll figure something out. Let's keep walking."

Printed in the United States
by Baker & Taylor Publisher Services